THE
Area
FILES
51

THE
Area51
FILES

JULIE BUXBAUM
Illustrations by LAVANYA NAIDU

DELACORTE PRESS

Text copyright © 2022 by Julie Buxbaum
Cover art and interior illustrations
copyright © 2022 by Lavanya Naidu

All rights reserved. Published in the United States by Delacorte Press, an imprint of Random House Children's Books, a division of Penguin Random House LLC, New York.

Delacorte Press is a registered trademark and the colophon is a trademark of Penguin Random House LLC.

Visit us on the Web! rhcbooks.com

Educators and librarians, for a variety of teaching tools, visit us at RHTeachersLibrarians.com

Library of Congress Cataloging-in-Publication Data
is available upon request.
ISBN 978-0-593-42946-4 (hardcover) — ISBN 978-0-593-42947-1 (lib. bdg.) — ISBN 978-0-593-42948-8 (ebook)

The text of this book is set in 12-point Sabon.
Interior design by Michelle Cunningham

Printed in the United States of America
3rd Printing
First Edition

*This one is for Elili and Luca,
my favorite goofballs in all the cosmos*
—J.B.

*To Maddy, my partner in crime and all
our adventures past, present and future that
live in books and outside of them*
—L.N.

THE Area51 FILES

WHAT HAPPENS IN AREA 51 STAYS IN AREA 51

UNCLE ANISH

ME, SKY PATEL-BAUM, age 12, orphan, loner, champion french-fries-dipped-in-ice-cream eater

UFO: Unidentified Food Object

SPIKE

Why flip-flops?

"SERIOUSLY, THAT'S IT. THAT'S THE MOST IMPORTANT RULE here." This is what my Uncle Anish says when I meet him for the very first time. He's wearing his full military uniform even though it's a Sunday. His chest gleams with medals, heavy and bright.

I wonder what he did to earn them.

Because I don't actually know my Uncle Anish.

In the twelve years I've been alive, he hasn't once called or texted or sent an email, but I guess that doesn't matter now. "Water under the bridge," as Grandma would say. Because suddenly, as of today, he is my new guardian.

Which means he's now the boss of me.

"Repeat the rule, please," he says.

"Um, what happens in Area 51 stays in Area 51?" I repeat. I wonder if I'm supposed to salute. Spike, my pet hedgehog, looks out through the bars of his cage, all poke-y and uncertain.

This is not because of my uncle or his serious uniform or the fact that we are currently the farthest we've ever been from home.

Spike always seems poke-y and uncertain.

By the time we were dropped just outside the gates of Area 51 this afternoon, we'd been in the car for almost ten hours. Long enough that I'd spotted license plates from all fifty states. By the time I found

Alaska, Spike had already filled three hedgehog diapers.

"Your grandma said not to jump to conclusions about you. That you look a mess but that you're as smart as your mom was. Is this true?" my Uncle Anish asks.

"Um, yeah, I guess," I say, and can't tell if that was an insult or a compliment. I have no way of knowing if I'm as smart as my mother was, but my report cards have always been good enough for Grandma to put them up on our refrigerator with magnets. And back in California, my teachers always liked me way better than my classmates did.

"So your grandma told you about all this, right?" my uncle asks nervously as he waves around at the little house we're standing in. It's tidy; there's no half-read books or half-drunk mugs of tea or half-eaten potato chip bags lying around like at my old house. It's very clear that this has been, until now, a no-kid zone. But I don't think he means the little house. He means everything else. As in the top-secret military base where he apparently lives and works. And where I live now, too, I guess.

We are, after all, in Area 51, a place where everything is so highly classified it's not even on the map.

OFFICIAL MAP

ULTRA-TOP-SECRET MAP

60 square miles

AREA 51

Almost three times the size of Manhattan!

"I guess," I say, and try to sound serious, despite the breakfast leftovers smeared on my shirt and the sounds of Spike's tiny feet scraping the bottom of his cage, and the weirdness of my being here at all.

I've heard the rumors about Area 51. That fifty years ago, UFOs (unidentified flying objects, not, you know, unidentified food objects) crash-landed here in the desert and that government scientists have been studying them ever since in secret underground labs. That these government scientists have proof that aliens exist.

Not that I believe them.

That would be ridiculous.

"I mean yes," I try again, all official-like. "Sir?"

"You can just call me Uncle Anish," he says, but I swear my "sir" makes him stand a little taller in his uniform, which I didn't think was possible, seeing as he is already the tallest man I've ever seen. He reminds me of the palm trees in Grandma's backyard, and how I have to bend my neck back to see the tops.

Thinking about the palm trees makes me think of Grandma. I already miss her even though we said goodbye only this morning.

I think about what Grandma might be doing right now—I picture her hanging laundry on the line—and

then I remember she's not in our tiny cottage by the ocean. She moved to that retirement home crammed like a new tooth into the center of town.

That's why I'm here in this bizarre place. Apparently kids aren't allowed to live in retirement homes. When I asked Grandma why kids were so disturbing to old people, she laughed.

"Too noisy," she said, using that voice she always uses when she means something different from what she says out loud.

I've lived with Grandma almost my entire life. See, I'm an orphan, which can sometimes feel weird because the only other orphans I've met in real life are grown-ups.

Not just grown-ups, but *old* grown-ups.

But there are lots of kid orphans in books, and kid orphans in books always have amazing adventures. I've been telling myself that moving in with Uncle Anish will be the start of mine. I'm convinced this is what my fifth-grade teacher called an *inciting incident*.

The plan for me to move in with my uncle, however, was always more than a little misleading. For example, until today I always thought my Uncle Anish was a paleontologist in South America. I thought I'd be joining him on a dinosaur bones expedition. That I wouldn't be able to call my grandma for a while because there wouldn't be cell service.

He is *not* a paleontologist in South America.

And as far as I know, there are no dinosaur bones here to dig up.

At least now I understand why Uncle Anish has never reached out to me before.

ALL THE THINGS BANNED IN AREA 51:

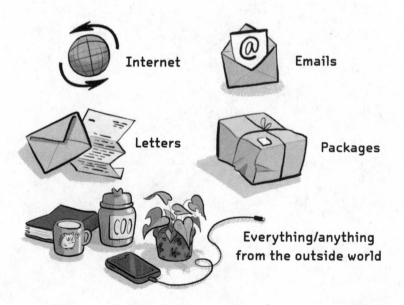

Internet

Emails

Letters

Packages

Everything/anything from the outside world

"Remember, no one can ever know this place exists," Uncle Anish says. "To the rest of the world, Area 51 is just a creepy old training base. They like to make wild guesses about what happens here. But they have no idea."

He sounds full of pride, like he built Area 51 with his own bare hands. I look around, but so far I haven't seen anything that interesting or impressive. On the golf cart ride from the security check to Uncle Anish's house, we took what Uncle Anish called the "back roads." I didn't see anything except a row of small pastel-colored homes with square yards of fake green grass.

"There is no other place like this on the entire planet. You have no idea how lucky you are," he says.

He's right about that. I don't feel lucky at all.

"Those of us who live and work in Area 51 devote our entire lives to studying unidentified aerial phenomena—what the average person would call UFOs—and, of course, the Break Throughs."

"Break Throughs?" I ask.

"Break Throughs are beings from other planets who have traveled here. Extraterrestrials. We call them Break Throughs because they've survived the transition through the Earth's atmosphere. And they live among us as our neighbors and friends."

"When you say 'Break Throughs,' do you mean . . . aliens?" I ask.

"Yes, in common parlance, aliens," Uncle Anish says. "In Area 51 there are lots and lots of aliens."

Wait, what?

TWO

NOT A TREE IN SIGHT

"YOUR GRANDMA DIDN'T MENTION THE HEDGEHOG," UNCLE Anish says, and drops a heavy, thick hardcover book titled *Area 51 Handbook* on the small kitchen table in front of me. It makes a loud, echoey thud.

Does Uncle Anish expect me to read that thing?

Not happening.

"Yeah, well, she didn't mention the aliens, either," I say, and glance around the little house. But I don't see any aliens—or, excuse me, "Break Throughs." I see only typical kitcheny things, like a refrigerator and a random assortment of chipped old-fashioned-looking dishes stacked in the glass-fronted cabinets.

Uncle Anish sits down across from me and examines me with the same intensity I examine him. I notice we have the same cheek dimple right under our left eyes.

Weird. When I first got here, I thought Grandma

had accidentally sent me to a prison. She had been cagey—no pun intended—about where I was going and how things would work in my new life. She'd promised that Uncle Anish would take good care of me and warned that since I'd be off-grid, we'd be out of touch for a while.

But I hadn't expected this.

Aliens? Seriously???

I was escorted to Area 51 in a vintage convertible, with a driver who didn't even look at me or Spike. As if he was very used to driving around hedgehogs in diapers.

There had been a series of signs as the car pulled closer and closer to the base.

First:

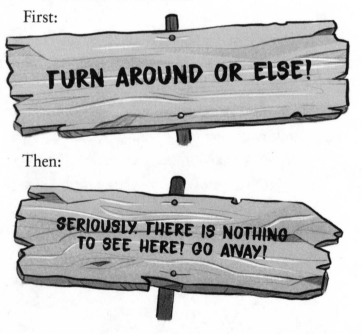

TURN AROUND OR ELSE!

Then:

SERIOUSLY, THERE IS NOTHING TO SEE HERE! GO AWAY!

Then:

WHAT ARE YOU STILL DOING HERE???

But the driver Uncle Anish had sent for me kept on going, as if he knew exactly where we were headed. He didn't even have a GPS. Not that there's cell service this far out in the desert.

My first view of Area 51 wasn't pretty. High glass walls surrounded the edges of the base, and barbed wire looped around on top of those.

THIS IS MOST DEFINITELY NOT AREA 51! I REPEAT: NOT AREA 51!

My first experiences here weren't pretty, either.

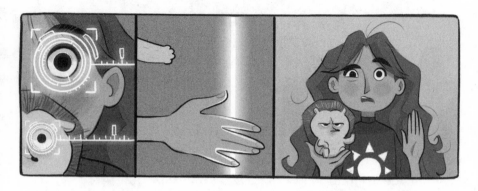

On this side, though, things feel friendlier. I like that Uncle Anish's house is pink, his neighbors' the pale blue of the sky on one side, lilac on the other. The sun shines hot and bright even though it's almost evening. There seems to be a surprising amount of fluorescent-painted buildings.

"Uncle Anish?" I finally say, breaking our intense eye contact. The words feel unfamiliar in my mouth, especially the *uncle* part. It's always been just Grandma and me, though she doesn't have a dimple. "Why aren't there any trees here? Is it because we're in the desert?"

"Good eye, kid. Excellent attention to detail. There are no plants at all in Area 51. All that oxygen bothers the Break Throughs."

"Huh," I say.

"Don't worry. You'll get used to it."

Spike scratches angrily at his cage. There's nothing Spike enjoys more than chasing squirrels up trees.

"It's okay, buddy. You'll find a new hobby," I tell him, and reach my finger between the bars to pet his nose.

Uncle Anish is still just sitting there awkwardly, so I open the Area 51 handbook to a page with a picture of a creature that looks like a hammerhead shark with legs. Next to it, there's a list:

FIVE FUN FACTS ABOUT BREAK THROUGHS AND AREA 51

1. All information about Area 51 is fully classified and must never be revealed to anyone off base or in the wider world.

2. Members of the Area 51 community, Break Throughs and humans alike, are not allowed to leave the base. Ever. Like not even once.

3. Species come in all shapes and sizes and have many interesting identifiable characteristics! The Audiotooters, for example, fart out of their ears and release a delightful whiff of roses.

4. In Area 51, we live by "no waste" principles,

and all items must be carefully reused or recycled.

5. All members of the 51 community come in peace and love and seek harmony.

I close the book quickly. Turns out we have different ideas of what a "fun fact" is. I'm not really a fan of looking at pictures of hammerhead sharks with legs. That possibly exist in real life. Within the sixty square miles in which I now currently live. A real fun fact would be like "On Fridays we have pajama day!"

Holy cannoli.

This can't be real.

"So just to be clear . . . you were joking about the aliens, right?" I ask Uncle Anish.

"I don't joke," Uncle Anish says. "Never learned how." He gestures me over to the window. "Here, come see."

I laugh, because I assume he is joking about not joking.

But nope. He is not joking about not joking.

Sorry to confuse you.

What I mean is he's totally serious.

I live in Area 51 now.

And no joke, there are aliens here.

Everywhere.

· · · THREE · · ·

RULE NUMBER 4: DO NOT LEAVE THE HOUSE

UNCLE ANISH, IT TURNS OUT, IS A VERY BUSY MAN. HIS official title is Deputy Head of the Federal Bureau of Alien Investigations, known as the FBAI, which he says means he's the second-in-command here.

Uncle Anish explained that the FBAI's most important responsibility is to keep the Break Through community in 51 safe and healthy. But apparently the FBAI is also in charge of studying Break Throughs. Its motto is "Learning and protecting the secrets of the universe."

It actually says that on the badge.

"Forget everything you've ever learned about our planet and our solar system. It's all wrong," Uncle Anish whispered last night, after dragging me outside to look at the stars even though both of us were already in our pajamas. "Our world is so much bigger than we ever knew. Don't be afraid.

The Break Throughs only come in peace. They are our friends."

This morning he was back to looking official in his uniform, with a walkie-talkie and a flashlight clipped to his belt. He told me he won't come home till late tonight. I get the impression that he's not used to taking care of a kid, because he doesn't even mention lunch. At least I have the granola bars Grandma packed for me.

I can't start school until I get a higher security clearance, but Uncle Anish claims he's working on it. In the meantime, I'm supposed to "lie low."

Lying low is **BORING.**

The problem is that because Area 51 is off the grid, there's no cable or satellites. Watching TV means watching the only channel on the base, which plays the same newscast from 1951 over and over.

So when Uncle Anish leaves for work, I snoop around his house, looking for I-don't-know-what. Pictures of my mom, maybe? Evidence that this whole thing is not a bizarre dream and I'm actually living in a land full of aliens?

To be honest, even if I hadn't just found myself in the strangest place on the planet, *literally,* I'd still be snooping.

My grandma calls me curious.

Everyone else calls me nosy.

It doesn't matter, though, because I find nothing except a pantry full of boxes of Cheerios and a closet full of FBAI jumpsuits. Unlike Grandma's house, there are no piles of papers and old magazines, no abandoned craft projects, no jars of peanut butter you're allowed to eat from with a spoon.

I'd happily spend the day looking out the front window watching the Break Throughs walk, glide, roll, fly, and jump by, but my uncle told me I needed to keep the blinds closed. He said we are currently on "high alert," whatever that means.

Spike and I are so bored we resort to playing hide-and-go-seek. I'm hiding in the closet when I first get the feeling someone is watching me. Not

Spike—I saw him scuffle into the kitchen and hop onto the counter. Spike isn't great with understanding spaces, so he's always looking for me in places much smaller than I can fit, like the drain in the bathroom sink. He once looked for me in Grandma's medicine cabinet, which can barely hold much more than a toothbrush.

But right now, while I hide in the closet, I can sense that someone else is here. I feel eyes on me as sharp as a laser.

I shiver in fear.

I crawl out of the front closet and grab one of Uncle Anish's shoes, the closest thing I can find to a weapon. I think of all the questions I should have asked before this moment: What do the aliens look like? Where do they fall on the Myers-Briggs personality test? Do they have superpowers? Will they eat me? Those questions suddenly seem much more important than the one I did ask Uncle Anish when I first got here: Where is the bathroom?

Spike doesn't hear me. He's too busy looking for me in the dishwasher. Hedgehogs make great best friends, but they are terrible in a crisis. I look around for a phone so I can call 911, and then I remember there are no phones in Area 51.

Think, Sky, think, I tell myself.

But there is no time for thinking, because when I look up, I finally see where the eyes are coming from.

Not an alien. Phew. A dog.

A giant fluffy dog looks at me through the small space between the blinds in the front windows. He has patchy black-and-white fur sticking out in all directions, like he just came out fresh from the dryer. His tongue lolls out of his mouth and his tail wags to a beat only he can hear. I break into a grin.

I jump up, drop the shoe, and run out the front door, immediately forgetting Uncle Anish's rule number 4: Do not leave the house. Apparently I need security clearance for that, too.

Attached to the dog is a leash, and attached to the leash is a boy. At first glance, at least, he looks to be a normal kid around my age. Light brown skin, a mess of short brown hair, and brown eyes.

Not scary, I tell myself.

Just another kid, I tell myself.

Until I notice he's wearing a yellow T-shirt that looks just like mine. But instead of a needlepoint sun on it, there's a picture of my grandma eating an ice cream cone.

What the heck?

It's impossible for him to have bought that shirt in a store. Are there even stores in Area 51?

Focus, Sky.

I start to roll up the sleeves of my sweatshirt because that's what kids who are about to fight do in movies. Who is this boy? How dare he wear a shirt with a picture of *my grandma*?

Seeing her face, especially in such an unexpected place, makes my stomach hurt. I still don't understand why I can't talk to or write to her. Why didn't she better prepare me for this?

Be brave and strong, she said.

Suddenly, I hate this place and everyone in it.

"Your shirt," I say.

"Excuse me?" the boy asks.

"Your shirt. Where did you get that?

"I am not wearing a shirt," he says, infuriatingly calm. He kneels next to his dog, who rolls over. The boy scratches the dog's belly, which the dog apparently likes, because he does a little dance along the floor. Head one way, bottom the other. I would find it adorable if I weren't currently so angry I could spit.

"You are! And that's my grandma!"

"You must be Agent Patel's niece, Sky. We heard you were coming. I'm your new neighbor. Have you been debriefed?"

"I haven't been debriefed, but you're about to be deshirted," I say.

The boy laughs, and I feel the heat rise in my cheeks.

"You're funny. I'm Elvis, and this is my dog, Pickles. Nice to meet you." The boy holds up his fingers in a peace sign. "I didn't steal your shirt. You are imagining me in it. That's how my species works. I shape-shift depending on who is looking at me. I'm a Break Through. You've heard about us, right?"

No way.

Can't be.

Am I talking to . . . an actual . . . alien?

Is this even real life?

"Um," I say, and it sticks in my throat. This can't be happening. It's one thing to have seen aliens outside Uncle Anish's window last night, which felt a bit like watching a cartoon come to life. It's a whole other thing to be chatting with an alien like it's no big deal.

"I see you only have security clearance one," Elvis says. I follow his eyes; there's a flashing hologram of the number one over my shoulder. How did that get there?

"We should go back inside before the authorities catch us," he says.

Authorities? Clearly Uncle Anish wasn't joking when he told me rule number 4. I assumed the rules were more like suggestions, sort of like how Grandma limits my screen time. Now I wonder what would happen if we got caught.

Spike totters out next to me and climbs up my leg, settling on my left shoulder. I know he's at full poke-y because I can feel his quills dig into my skin. I'm frozen in place.

"Come on. We have to hurry," Elvis says, and walks right into Uncle Anish's house. I look at Spike, who has skidded down my arm, leaving lines of scratches.

Spike might be terrible in a crisis, but he's a good judge of character. I look at him and silently ask him what I should do.

Spike nods at me, so I follow Elvis inside.

· · · FOUR · · ·

SOMETHING WEIRD
GOING ON AROUND HERE

I'M SITTING ON UNCLE ANISH'S COUCH WITH A STRANGE boy who's wearing a T-shirt with a picture of my grandma on it and who I'm 95 percent sure is not actually human.

This. Is. So. Weird.

"Is the dog . . ." I don't know the polite way of saying *Is your dog a dog or an alien I somehow see as a dog?* but Elvis seems to understand my question without my having asked.

Stay curious, Grandma said.

"Pickles is a real dog. *Canis lupus familiaris.* Common household pet for Earthlings," Elvis says. "He is not the snack or the hamburger garnish made from fermented cucumbers."

"Right."

"And your hedgehog's name?" Elvis asks.

"Spike," I say. "He's a real hedgehog."

"Did you know his quills are made of keratin, the same biological material as human fingernails and hair?" he asks.

"Yeah," I say. "I did."

"Sorry. Galzorian brain capacity is a bit bigger than humans', but Agent Patel said you're smart. We absorb and savor interesting factoids the same way your kind absorb Doritos."

"Right," I say again, squinting at him. I turn my head to one side to see if he looks different from that angle. Nope. Still a boy wearing a T-shirt with my grandma's face.

"Am I going to get in trouble for going outside and for having you in here?" I ask. I have a gazillion questions on the tip of my tongue, but this is the one that wins. I wonder why I'm not allowed to leave the house when Uncle Anish promised me that the Break Throughs aren't dangerous.

"You went back inside fast enough. Seventy-three more seconds and the alarm would have tripped. Don't worry. Break Throughs are encouraged to socialize with humans. Even Level Ones. It's part of the Area 51 experiment. But you do need security clearance to wander freely."

When Pickles barks at him, Spike barks back. Well, not barks exactly, because he's a hedgehog, but

he does the hedgehog equivalent of barking. I'd call it a purr, but I know Spike gets mad when I use that word.

"Look! They're making friends. Like we are," Elvis says, and holds up his hand again in a peace sign. I'm still learning alien etiquette, but I peace-sign back. Elvis grins at me, and I decide I kind of like this kid. Or alien. Or whatever.

"Yeah," I say.

"Can I trust you?" Elvis asks, suddenly a little nervous. I nod. "I take that as an affirmative."

"Yes."

"Something weird is going on around here lately."

"Something weird?" I ask, because I can't think of anything weirder than what is currently happening or than this place existing at all.

WEIRD THINGS CURRENTLY HAPPENING:

1. Sky is chatting with an alien and his non-alien dog in Uncle Anish's house in Area 51.

2. Sky is hundreds of miles from home.

3. ALIENS! ALIENS! ALIENS!

"A bunch of Break Throughs went missing at the exact moment you arrived yesterday," Elvis says, and I take a second to let that sink in. The words *the exact moment you arrived* sound . . . I don't know . . . ominous.

"Break Throughs like you?" I ask.

"Not my kind. A sister planet. From Zdstram-maroos. This is a HUGE deal."

"Why?"

"Break Throughs don't suddenly go missing in 51. We're closely tracked. Rule number seven: No one goes in or out of 51. You are the first person to move to 51 in over five years. And this is the first time Break Throughs have gone missing in almost a decade," Elvis says, talking more quickly, as if he needs to get it all out fast. "I don't think people will see this as a coincidence."

"Maybe the aliens from Zdstra-whatever just left," I say.

"They're called Zdstrammars from the planet Zdstrammaroos," Elvis corrects me.

"Zdstrammars," I repeat.

"You can't just leave Area 51," Elvis says, and although this isn't new information, I don't love being reminded of it.

"Right. Rule seven. So what do you think happened?" I ask. I can't help but be curious despite not being sure I want to know the answer. I am still just getting used to the idea that Break Throughs actually exist—not to mention the fact that I am, right at this moment, talking to one.

My brain hurts.

"I think the Zdstrammars were kidnapped," Elvis says.

"Kidnapped?!"

And just like that, I wonder if brains can actually explode.

· · · FIVE · · ·

CODE 61154, ON THE DOUBLE

AFTER ELVIS AND PICKLES RETURN TO THE LILAC HOUSE NEXT door, Uncle Anish walks in looking tired and sweaty. Even his medals seem to be drooping. When he sees me sitting on the couch, he looks surprised, like he forgot I existed.

"Hi," I say.

"Oh hey, Sky. Sorry, long day," he says, and slumps into the chair across from me.

Uncle Anish looks stressed. And maybe even a little bit scared.

I guess Elvis is right, and these missing Zdstrammars are a really big deal.

I wonder if I'll ever understand things here in Area 51.

"Do you want me to make you some dinner?" I ask, thinking about the limited food I've seen in the pantry. I could pour us bowls of Cheerios. Maybe if

I feed him he'll perk up, and if he perks up he can explain what's going on.

"Nah, I ate in the mess hall. Wait, what about you? Shoot, things have been so bananas around here I forgot to get you food!" Uncle Anish stands up and hits himself in the forehead. "What have you been eating?" he asks.

"Grandma packed me granola bars," I say.

"And that's all you've had all day?" He looks frantic now, and grabs his walkie-talkie. I shrug. I like granola bars, especially the ones with chocolate in them.

Uncle Anish is so tall that when he sits back down his shins look like a toddler slide.

Code 61154, on the double. I repeat, Code 61154, OTD.

"What's Code 61154?" I ask.

"Pizza," he says, like it is the most obvious thing in the world.

☢ ☢ ☢

Turns out pizza in Area 51 is exactly the same as pizza in California, except it's delivered by a drone. We eat outside in the back at a wooden picnic table under the same twinkling lights Grandma had at home. Apparently my security clearance allows me to hang out in the backyard but not the front.

"As you can tell, I'm new to this," Uncle Anish says, and holds his palms out.

"New to what?" I ask.

"Parenting. Or Uncle-ing. Or whatever," Uncle Anish says.

"Well, I'm new to this too. I've never nieced before," I say. Uncle Anish laughs, and I feel something inside me relax.

I squint, try to see him as someone other than a stranger.

We are related.

We have the same strange fold in our ears, like we hear out of envelopes.

That must mean something, right?

Who knows?

"I think we'll figure out this uncle-niece thing. Work has been a little difficult at the FBAI," Uncle Anish says. My stomach twists again. "I've been distracted since you came."

He says this last bit as if talking to himself and not to me. Is this all my fault?

"Elvis told me some of what's been happening. I can stay out of your way. I'm sorry if me coming here has caused problems for you," I say.

"Oh no, Sky! That's not what I meant!" Uncle Anish exclaims.

How do three Zdstrammars just disappear?

What we know so far: The Zs disappeared at 2:54 p.m., the exact same moment Sky arrived. What we don't know: EVERYTHING ELSE.

"We have one rule here," Uncle Anish says. "Actually, that's not true. We have tons of rules here, but there is only one super-duper-important rule."

"What happens in Area 51 stays in Area 51," I repeat, and feel my insides shiver. This super-duper-important rule makes me feel a little ill.

"Right. So that's basically our way of saying

there's no leaving. Especially not for Break Throughs. I'm worried that if the missing Zs somehow went off base they could be seriously injured, or even . . ." Uncle Anish doesn't finish his sentence. He shudders.

"You'll find them," I say.

"The timing couldn't be worse, either. I'm supposed to be promoted to the head of the FBAI next month. The medal ceremony is all planned—though maybe not now, after everything—" Uncle Anish gets cut off by a siren in the distance that starts as a low hum and quickly gets louder.

Stay low. Get under the table.

No, it's not one siren. It must be hundreds. Red lights stream across the yard, and the alarms continue to blare. I crawl under the table, and Spike, who has been sharing my pizza, reluctantly drops his piece and joins me. Then he changes his mind, sticks out one paw to grab his dropped sliced, and scurries back next to me. He stuffs it greedily into his mouth.

"What's happening?" I ask, but Uncle Anish doesn't respond. He's yelling into his walkie-talkie. I hear the chop of helicopters. Because there are no trees here, only long fields of artificial grass, you can see into everyone else's backyards. The helicopters' white beams move from house to house. They are obviously looking for someone. Or something.

"Sorry. I need to go, but I'll be back as soon as possible. Hurry. Go inside and lock the door." Uncle Anish throws me his keys and then sprints away to his golf cart.

And just like that, Spike and I are alone again.

SIX

GET IN THE HATCHES!

SPIKE AND I STAY UNDER THE TABLE FOR A FEW MINUTES, mostly because I'm too scared to move. It feels safe here, where we can see what's happening but where presumably no one can see us.

I hear sniffling and feel something wet at my back. I jump and bump my head on the table. I turn around, and there's Pickles with his tongue out, his tail wagging.

"Sorry! Sorry!" Elvis says, running up. "I dropped his leash."

"Shhh," I say, and motion for Elvis to get down and join us under the table. He looks the same—like a friendly boy—but he's no longer wearing a T-shirt with a picture of Grandma on it. Instead, he's wearing a green sweatshirt with a drawing of Spike in the center. I point to it, eyebrows raised.

"I have no idea what you are seeing, but just

know it's your projection of what you think I look like, not what I actually look like," Elvis says.

"I don't get it."

"The human mind can't comprehend my form. It's outside the normal three-dimensional paradigm. And so you use your own imagination to fill in my details to make something you are comfortable with."

Why do you wear T-shirts with pictures of my favorite things?

That means your soul trusts my soul.

I'm not sure what to say. I've never considered my soul, much less Elvis's soul—do aliens even have souls?—but with sirens blaring and the fact that we are currently hiding under a picnic table, now is not the time to get into it.

Maybe it's true. I do trust him. Maybe even more than I trust Uncle Anish, who abandoned me faster than you can call a Code 61154.

I hold my fingers up in a peace sign, and Elvis grins.

"Wait, so are your facial expressions also manifested by me? Like when I think you are smiling are you actually smiling?" I'm suddenly very worried that this whole friendship is a figment of my imagination.

Back in California, Grandma said that maybe I wasn't great at making friends because I had different interests than my classmates. I always thought it was because I *was* different from my classmates.

Orphans with pet hedgehogs don't exactly grow on trees at my old school, Yawn Middle.

Could Elvis's impossible-to-see form be frowning at me?

"No! Of course I control my own facial signals!" Elvis seems super offended by this idea. "Such a common human misconception. Just because I am a Break Through doesn't mean I don't have feelings!"

"Okay. Sorry," I say, shrugging. The alarm suddenly switches to a pattern of beeps, which makes the alarm even more alarming.

Hmmm. Didn't know that was possible.

Bing-bong, bing-bong, bing-bing-bing-bong.

"What does that mean?" I ask.

"It's the signal to get in the hatches. Come on!" Elvis says. "Agent Patel's hatch is closest!"

"Hatch?" I ask. "What's a hatch? Also, do scary alarms always go off around here?"

But Elvis doesn't answer my questions. Instead, he grabs Pickles's leash and runs into Uncle Anish's house, this time through the back door, making it clear that I'm supposed to follow. I peek out from under the table, scoop up Spike, who happens to still be holding the pizza box, look both ways, though I don't even know what I'm looking for—aliens? the FBAI to come arrest me? a drone attack?—and run inside.

SEVEN

SECRET CODES AND ALARMING ALARMS

ELVIS IS STRONGER THAN HE LOOKS. HE CASUALLY PICKS UP Uncle Anish's old television set—one of those clunky square boxes with rabbit ears that look like they're from when dinosaurs roamed the earth—and places it on the floor. He then twists the table the TV was sitting on—which is bolted into the floor—as if it is a wheel.

Step back.

Houses in Area 51 have secret hatches!

"What are you doing?" The last thing I need is for Elvis to trash the house and then for Uncle Anish to throw me out. Would the authorities let me get on a plane to California if that happened?

Nope. What happens in Area 51 stays in 51.

Uncle Anish has made it clear: I'm not allowed to leave. No one is.

I gulp.

I've seen Elvis, and could therefore take that classified information with me.

I think about those memory-erasing blasters you see in movies, and for the first time in my life, I hope they are real. That's the only thing I can think of right now that could get me out of this mess.

Then again, Grandma sold our cottage.

There isn't a home for me to go back to, whether my memory is erased or not.

"I'm opening the hatch," Elvis says. And sure enough, the floor beneath the table begins to turn. "What do you think Agent Patel's secret code is?"

"What do you mean? Secret code?" I ask.

"This works like a locker combination. Four digits. So give me some ideas to try. Hurry. What's Agent Patel's birthday?"

"No idea," I say. "I just met him."

"Your birthday, then?" Elvis asks.

"His code is not going to be my birthday. Did you not hear me? We just met two days ago," I say.

I hear a bark and see that Spike is sitting on Pickles's back and Pickles is chasing his tail to shake him off. Spike is clearly winning whatever game they are playing.

"But Agent Patel knew about you before then, of course. You're all he's talked about for as long as I've known him. He used to tell me that you'd come live here in your twelfth Earth-year and that you and I were going to be good friends," Elvis says.

"Uncle Anish talked about me?" I ask.

"Of course. He even showed me a picture! Not sure how he got it, with the nothing-in-or-out-of-51 rule. But he has one. He keeps it in his wallet. In it, your hair's all . . ." Elvis does a hurricane motion around his head, or maybe it's a tornado. Whatever. He means messy.

I want to ask more about the picture, but the alarms are continuing to blare their strange rhythm.

Man, these alarms are still very alarming.

"Wow," I say.

"What's your birthday?" Elvis asks again.

"December fourteenth."

"Okay, so one, two, one, four." Elvis turns the table right one time, left twice, right again one time, left four times. And like magic, I hear a click, and the table turns on its side to reveal an opening in the floor. Below, a ladder unfolds itself.

Uncle Anish's secret code is *my* birthday. Huh.

"Come on," Elvis says, and though for a half second I wonder if it's a good idea to follow an alien I've known for fewer than twenty-four hours into a secret hatch hidden below Uncle Anish's floor, I decide I have no choice. "Seriously! Get in! This alarm is the highest alert level. Go!"

Desperate times call for desperate measures.

"Spike!" I call. I climb down first, then Elvis, then Pickles with Spike on his back.

"Whoa," I say, when we reach the bottom and I look around. "Holy cannoli."

EIGHT

AT LEAST THE GALZORIA ARE FRIENDLY

"DOES EVERY HOUSE HAVE A HATCH LIKE THIS?" I ASK Elvis. I don't have a phone or an iPad—all my electronics were confiscated that first day at the security hut—but I'd guess we've been down here at least an hour. The door above us is shut, the ladder folded back up on itself, and when it all closed, it made the sort of click that makes me think it is locked.

We are likely stuck here until Uncle Anish comes home and finds us.

I wonder how long that will be.

"Yes. Every house is equipped with a hatch with its own code. If you read your *Area 51 Handbook*, you'd know that we have a variety of alarms here. *Bing-bong, bing-bong, bing-bing-bing-bong* translates to 'Get in your hatch, on the double!'"

I forgot about my *Area 51 Handbook*.

In my defense, it's the sort of book you instinctively ignore. Clearly Uncle Anish should have said, *Read this, it has emergency codes you need to know to survive here. Otherwise you might die!* Then I would have at least flipped through it beyond the creepy shark-man thingy.

"This place is so bizarre." I mean the hatch, but

I guess it applies to Area 51 too. We are in a giant basement that has a single lightbulb hanging from a string in the ceiling. A large machine is built into the wall, and it emits a staticky sound, like a radio between stations. "What's the big emergency? Why did we need to get in here?"

"The walkie-talkie said that there was possibly another missing Break Through. But that's all I heard."

"*Someone else was kidnapped?*" I ask.

"I think so," Elvis says. "Want a snack?"

I feel whiplash at the abrupt subject change. Elvis opens the giant fridge, the first thing I've seen in Area 51 that doesn't look like it's from fifty years ago. This one is the kind that was on the cover of those home decoration magazines Grandma liked. Big and silver with panes of glass so you can see inside. I wish I'd known about this place earlier, because I would have definitely skipped Grandma's broken granola bars. Uncle Anish is fully stocked with candy, soda, chocolate, and a variety of prepared meals that are labelled *RTE,* which Elvis explains means ready-to-eat.

We could stay down here for years and not go hungry.

This thought is reassuring until I realize that's the point of this place.

I start to feel a little nauseated.

"No thanks," I say. Elvis grabs a Hershey bar and eats it in two quick bites. So that answers another question I didn't know I wanted to ask until I saw it answered: I guess aliens eat food just like humans.

I wander over to a wall covered with posters. They are fascinating. They remind me of my sixth-grade science classroom, and how Mrs. Oodleboodlebaum liked to cover her walls with information so that when our eyes drifted from her at the front of the room, we'd still be learning.

These posters are drawings of various types of aliens, with their family name written below and their defining characteristics. I walk around, absorbing as much as I can.

"Which one are you?" I ask Elvis, who has come to stand beside me. The forms vary widely. A few look exactly what I imagined aliens looked like before all this: green and round with antennae and googly eyes, like the alien magnet on Grandma's fridge. Most don't look like beings at all.

One is an assortment of circles stuck together, like microscopic cells.

Another is a row of straight vertical lines, like rulers marching.

I look in awe. It turns out Break Throughs come in every shape and size imaginable, and even unimaginable: tiny dinosaurs, giant jellyfish, toddler-sized worms, creatures with eyeballs all around the crowns of their heads, women who have built-in pockets in their thighs. The most human-like creature, which looks almost kid-like, has finned hands and wheels for feet.

Elvis points to a poster all the way on the left. The image of Elvis—or not Elvis himself, but Elvis's species—reminds me of a lava lamp. Globular liquid mixing together in rainbow colors. I look at Elvis, who blinks at me, and then I look back at the picture.

No resemblance whatsoever.

Creepy.

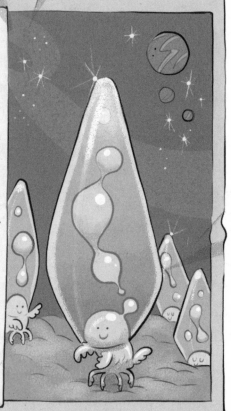

FAMILY NAME: Galzoria

DEFINING CHARACTERISTICS: Picture not fully representative because 8-dimensional with oozing edges and therefore beyond limitations of human imagination. Form reactive to surroundings and viewer.

LIFE SPAN: 105 Earth-years. No mature Break Throughs in Area 51.

POPULATION IN AREA 51: 3 (extinction threat, current population all unrelated; unaccompanied minors, aged 12, 5, and 4)

HOSTILE OR FRIENDLY: Friendly

"Well, at least this tells me you're friendly," I say.

"Yes. It's official!" Elvis says, and shakes his fingers in jazz hands. I laugh.

I'm not yet ready to think about the fact that there are only three of Elvis's kind here and the other two are not his parents.

I know what that sort of loneliness feels like. I felt like I was the only one of my kind back at Yawn Middle.

Elvis leads me to a poster on the other side of the wall, the alien species that looks like a collection of bubbles. "Three of the Zdstrammar family went missing. Maybe one more tonight," he says sadly.

FAMILY NAME: Zdstrammar

DEFINING CHARACTERISTICS: Round edges, made up of a collection of at least 1,348 bubbles

LIFE SPAN: Data still being collected, but best estimate: 903 Earth-years. Both mature and infant specimens in Area 51. Mature unaffected by Earth's barriers.

POPULATION IN AREA 51: 657

HOSTILE OR FRIENDLY: Friendly

"When the alarm went off tonight, my parents grabbed their walkies and went immediately to headquarters. I can't remember the last time that happened," Elvis says. "The entire purpose of the FBAI is to track the alien population and keep them safe. Break Throughs understand that it would be impossible to leave Area 51 without getting hurt. Not only because of all the trees and plants on planet Earth, but because of the hysteria they'd cause among humans. That's why this is such a big deal."

"Huh," I say, not quite understanding.

"In the 1990s, some Retinayas—a species that has *a lot* of eyeballs—jumped the fence and were killed almost immediately by terrified Nevadians. Since then, the Break Throughs have been content to learn about Earth from the friendly humans in Area 51. They know the wider planet is unsafe for them."

"Wait, back up. You have parents?" I ask, and then wonder if this is why I didn't have friends back in California. I ask rude, possibly irrelevant questions. Elvis doesn't seem to mind, though.

"Yes. Adopted human parents. They're both agents, and my grandma is head of the FBAI. In Area 51, they pair all young unaccompanied Break Throughs with grown-ups. I lost what you would call my biological parents on entry. Adult Galzoria have trouble transitioning to the Earth's atmosphere."

"I'm sorry. I lost my parents when I was a baby," I say.

Elvis holds out a finger to me and I touch my

fingertip to his, E.T.–style. It's an odd gesture, but I understand its meaning deep in my bones: I have felt what you have felt.

"Do you remember yours? I mean your biological parents?" I ask.

"Memory works differently for Galzoria. We don't input in the same way. But yes and no. Yes, in that I can feel that they are part of me. No, in that I can't imagine them. You?"

"No. I was only three months old when they died. But sometimes I talk to them and pretend they can hear me." As soon as I say this, I realize this is not something I've ever said out loud. Not even to Grandma.

And just like that, I know I've made my first real friend. It doesn't seem to matter that he's not human.

"Who knows? Maybe they can hear you," Elvis says. He grabs a Snickers bar from the fridge, eats it, and then grabs another. "We may know more about the universe in Area 51 than any other place on Earth, but there's still a whole lot we don't understand."

"So how old are you now?" I ask.

"I'm also twelve in Earth-years, though my central processing center operates at a different age level."

"Central processing center?"

"My brain," Elvis says.

"Okay, so where does your central processing center think the missing Zdstrammars are?" I ask.

Elvis shrugs.

"I don't know. But I think we should figure it out."

"We?" I ask.

"Why not us?" Elvis asks.

I also have a central processing center. Mine says, "PIZZA! PIZZA! PIZZA!"

I TOO HAVE A CENTRAL PROCESSING CENTER: MINE SAYS, "SPIKE! SPIKE! SPIKE!"

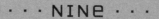

NINE

DON'T LET THE ELECTRODES SCARE YOU

WHEN I WAKE UP, IT TAKES ME A MINUTE TO REMEMBER where I am: Uncle Anish's weird hatch with my new alien friend. Right. You know, just a normal Monday morning.

"We were so worried," a woman's voice says from behind one of the flashlights currently being beamed into my face. She's white, and looks to be the same age as Uncle Anish, probably early forties. Her swishy blond hair is tied into a high ponytail. She's wearing a blue jumpsuit with the letters *FBAI* stitched above the pocket. She grabs Elvis into a hug, and Pickles jumps up and starts spinning in joyous circles. Pickles probably also thought we'd be stuck in here forever.

"Hi, Mom," Elvis says.

"Buddy, you can't just leave and not tell us where you're going. You know the rules," an Asian American man says. He's also wearing a blue jumpsuit. He sounds stern, but he's smiling and hugging Elvis too. It's clear that Elvis won the parent lottery.

"Sorry for splitting last night, Sky. We had a Code Red," says Uncle Anish, who appears behind them. He does not hug me, because we're still practically strangers, but at least he drops his flashlight so it's no longer shining in my eyes.

Maybe Elvis's parents can adopt me, too.

UNCLE ANISH: Like me, not so much a hugger. Like me, human.

LAUREN: Elvis's mom. Enthusiastic hugger, human.

MICHAEL: Elvis's dad. Also an enthusiastic hugger, also human.

"Sky! We are so happy to meet you. Your uncle gushes about you all the time," Lauren, Elvis's mom, says when she finally releases me. I look up at Uncle

Anish, but he doesn't meet my eyes. "You need anything here in 51, you come to us, or to Elvis. We're practically family."

"Thank you," I say.

"Is it true another Z went missing?" Elvis asks.

"Fortunately, it was a false alarm," Lauren says.

"Let's talk about this later. Sky, we've got to get you to headquarters really early so you can get cleared for school before class starts," Uncle Anish says. "It's time for your lie detector test. If you pass—"

"*When* she passes," Lauren interrupts.

"Right, *when* you pass, you'll be able to go straight to 51 Middle School." Uncle Anish says this as if it's a good thing. I'm not so sure. School has never been my jam, and I can't imagine here in Area 51, where half the kids are aliens, it will be much better.

Stranger, yes. Not necessarily better.

"A lie detector test?" I ask. My throat feels dry and itchy. I look longingly at the soda in the fridge and wonder if Uncle Anish is the kind of guardian who will let me have soda for breakfast. One look at Lauren and I know she definitely wouldn't.

"Don't worry. The test is easy as pie," Michael says. I've never heard that expression, "easy as pie." Does it mean as easy as eating pie, which, cool, I can do that? Or as easy as making pie, in which case, I'm screwed?

"The key is not to let the electrodes make you nervous, dear," Lauren says, and so that's when I start to freak out.

TeN

RELAX—THEY JUST READ YOUR BRAIN WAVES

HEADQUARTERS IS IN A COLOSSAL BUILDING THAT'S A FIVE- minute golf cart ride from Uncle Anish's house. There are no cars allowed in Area 51. When I ask Uncle Anish why, he grimaces and tells me it makes it too easy to smuggle things in and out. I wonder if he's thinking about the missing Zdstrammars.

The soda that I did end up drinking for breakfast—yup, turns out Uncle Anish is a pushover—sits uneasily in my stomach, and my nerves buzz from the caffeine.

Also turns out: soda for breakfast is a bad idea.

FBAI headquarters is the coolest building I've ever seen. It looks like something out of a children's fairy tale mashed with the Batcave's laboratory. There are high ceilings, and people wandering around in lab coats. The back wall is made of stained glass, and as we move closer, I see that glass forms an image of a giant ant—must be some sort of alien—reaching an antenna toward a human's hand.

Uncle Anish uses a full-body scanner to open the first set of doors, and once we are inside, a man in a blue FBAI jumpsuit asks me for my name. He then scans my fingertips, and when the machine bleeps, he says, "Toes, too."

I look up at Uncle Anish and he nods, as if this is normal procedure. I take off my shoes and socks and stand on another scanner, this one presumably recording my toeprints.

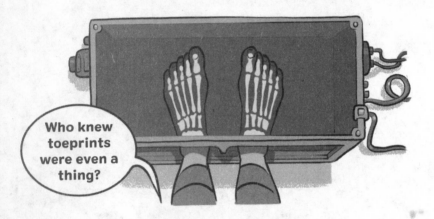

Who knew toeprints were even a thing?

The security guard seems satisfied and waves us through another set of doors, where a robotic voice instructs us to step up and look into a square box. I glance at Uncle Anish.

"Retinal scan," he tells me, and when I look confused he says, "They want to identify you by your eyeballs."

Well, that's just . . . disturbing. I wish Spike were

here. He'd make this all feel a tiny bit less scary, like he did the first day we got here.

"Do you have to do this every day?" I ask Uncle Anish.

"Yup. It's why I wear flip-flops," he says.

And just like that, at least one mystery of Area 51 is solved. Only 5,897,937 left to figure out.

Uncle Anish leads me to a room where two men stand waiting. One is short and stocky, with silver hair sticking straight in the air. He looks like a Troll doll. The other is taller, with absurdly bushy brows. He reminds me of Bert from *Sesame Street,* except not friendly.

TROLL
(not his real name)

BERT FROM
SESAME STREET
(also not his real name)

Not sure why both of these men's hair defies gravity.

A large machine with multicolored wires sits on the table. I no longer feel like I'm in a cool, happy building. Instead, this place feels cold, like a police station. If I get questions wrong, what will happen? Will they take me away from Uncle Anish?

"Sky, have a seat and we'll get started," the Troll says, and smiles in that condescending way grown-ups sometimes do at kids. I notice he's one of those people who spit when they talk and I feel a drop of wetness on my cheek. Ew. "I'm Agent Belcher. This is my partner, Agent Fartz."

I start to laugh, and Uncle Anish gives me a stern look.

"That's Fartz with a *Z*," the guy who looks like Bert says. Uncle Anish shakes his head, like he's disappointed in me for laughing. I shake my head back, like I'm disappointed he doesn't understand how hilarious this is.

Also, I'm nervous. When I'm nervous, I giggle.

No. It's not nerves.

It's that his name is Agent Fartz!

"Have a seat. I'm just going to attach these electrodes to your head," Agent Belcher says, and I look again at Uncle Anish, half expecting him to

LET'S TRY THIS AGAIN.

AGENT BELCHER

AGENT FARTZ.
(Get wind of this:
that's his real
name!)

object. I assumed they'd put them on my wrist, not my scalp.

"Relax. They just read your brain waves. No big deal," Uncle Anish says, and I feel shaky as I realize he's lying. It is a big deal. At least, it is for me. It's ten a.m. on a Monday. In my real life, I'd be in English class, having started my morning with a balanced breakfast that Grandma made for me before school.

Probably something that looks disgusting but tastes delicious, like oatmeal.

For the first time, I wonder if I can trust Uncle

Anish. He shouldn't have let me have soda for breakfast or abandoned me during an emergency.

Area 51 is too strange a place to trust *anyone*. I need to be more careful, keep my wits about me.

I can make out my reflection in the glass window in the door and my first thought is that I look like an alien.

I feel the giggles rise again.

I now know what aliens actually look like, and this is not it.

Nope, I look way weirder than normal aliens.

· · · ELEVEN · · ·

WHAT I LEARNED FROM NANCY DREW

"STATE YOUR NAME FOR THE RECORD," AGENT FARTZ SAYS, and I consider joking around. I could call myself Agent Poopz or something, but already know I won't get a laugh.

"Sky Patel-Baum," I say, and a machine that is drawing lines starts to make a loud whooshing sound as its needle goes up and down wildly, registering this as a lie. "Wait, sorry. My name is Priya Patel-Baum. It's just everyone calls me Sky."

The machine chills out. Phew.

"Why do people call you Sky?" Agent Fartz asks.

"My grandma said that when I was a baby, all I wanted to do was look up at the sky. I guess it just stuck as a nickname," I say.

"And when did you first hear about Area 51?" Agent Belcher asks.

"I mean, I read about this place a few years ago,

but I didn't know it was real or anything. I didn't know Uncle Anish lived here. My grandma told me I was moving to my uncle's last week," I say. The machine draws a flat line, which I assume means it knows I'm telling the truth.

"Where did you think your uncle, Agent Anish Patel, lived before you found out about Area 51?" Agent Fartz asks. His tone is colder than Agent Belcher's, and it feels like they may be playing good cop/bad cop.

"Grandma had always been pretty vague about it. She said he lived in South America or something. Grandma said he was off the grid, which was why he never called or FaceTimed or wrote or reached out." I look at Uncle Anish, and he nods, like *good job*.

"Did you believe her?" Agent Fartz asks.

"Umm." I pause. I can hear my heart thumping in my chest. "No."

"Really? Why not?" Uncle Anish asks, and Agent Fartz gives him a dirty look, like *I'm the one asking the questions around here*.

"Really? Why not?" Agent Fartz repeats.

"I don't know. I guess I just assumed he was dead. Like my parents." The two agents stare at the machine, which continues its straight line, but Uncle Anish looks at me like I've punched him in the gut.

"I'm sorry. I mean, who lives so far away they can't even send a birthday card?"

"Do you understand now why I couldn't write? Are you angry with me?" Uncle Anish asks, and though Agent Fartz seems about to interrupt again, Agent Belcher holds him back. I'm not sure I want to have this conversation with electrodes attached to my head, but I have no choice.

"I'm not angry, but I'm . . ." I stop, wait for the right word, knowing the machine will whirr if I don't say what I mean. "This is hard. We're strangers. And I miss Grandma."

My eyes fill with tears, and Uncle Anish puts his hand on my shoulder.

"No touching the test taker," Agent Fartz says.

"Relax," Agent Belcher says, landing another tiny bit of spit near my left eye. I wonder if it would be rude to wipe it off. "Give them a minute. She's a kid."

"I'm okay. We can keep going," I say. I want my uncle to know I'm tough. That's the one good thing about being an orphan: it has made me resilient.

"Did you have anything to do with the Zdstrammars that went missing?" Agent Belcher asks. He says it kindly, like it would not be a big deal if I did, though of course it totally would. I may be new to Area 51, but I wasn't born yesterday.

Also, why is he asking me this? How could I have had anything to do with it? Am I a suspect?!

"Nope," I say

No whooshing sound. Thank goodness.

"Do you have any knowledge of your uncle helping the Zdstrammars disappear?"

"Nope," I say, confused. Is Uncle Anish a suspect?!

"Fartz," Agent Belcher says in a warning tone, and I make a mental note that Agent Belcher seems to be on our side. Fartz obviously is not. Does Agent Fartz really think we would have anything to do with the aliens going missing?

I've read a million Nancy Drew books, and consider myself something of a sleuth. When you're trying to solve a mystery, the first thing you look for is motive. As far as I can tell, Uncle Anish has every reason for *not* wanting the Zdstrammars to disappear. After all, his job depends on it.

"And for the rest of your life, will you follow

the rules and restrictions read to you by Agent Patel on your arrival? First and foremost, what happens in Area 51 stays in Area 51?" Agent Belcher asks, ignoring Fartz.

"Yes," I say, and hold my breath waiting for the machine to make a noise.

I have no idea if I'm telling the truth. I don't plan to broadcast to the world what I know about Area 51. As Elvis explained, if people knew about Elvis and the rest of the Break Throughs, they'd try to hurt them.

People are usually scared of the things they don't understand.

I would never want to do anything to hurt my new friend. Still, can I keep this all secret forever? Am I expected to live the rest of my life in Area 51, which according to Elvis covers approximately sixty square miles?

Sure sounds like it.

It turns out I'm a good secret keeper, because the machine stays calm.

· · · TWELVE · · ·

UNCLE ANISH MIGHT HAVE A MOTIVE AFTER ALL

AFTER I PASS MY LIE DETECTOR TEST, THE VERY FIRST THING I do is lie: I tell Uncle Anish I need to use the bathroom and that I'll meet him out in front of the building when I'm finished. Really I just want to check out FBAI headquarters and see if I can get any more info on these missing Zdstrammars.

Elvis is right. We need to find them.

I peek through the rectangle window in the doors as I make my way down the halls. I see one room full of equipment with blinking lights, another filled with 3-D models of the aliens on the posters I saw in the hatch, another with screens showing images of both humans and aliens with the words *Wanted: Dead or Alive* flashing above their heads. After a few minutes, I realize I must have gone in a circle, because I'm back at the room we started in and I hear voices I recognize: Agent Belcher and Agent Fartz.

I stay as low as I can. I can still see them, but I don't think they can see me.

"How far did they track the Zdstrammar urine?" Agent Belcher asks.

Urine? They found urine? As in, you know, tinkle? Wait, aliens pee?

"Quarter mile up the road from the fence. It stops suddenly. The perp must have realized they were intentionally leaking," Agent Fartz says. I tuck this new information into my brain, remind myself to share it with Elvis later.

This feels important.

Our first clue!

My sleuthing Spidey senses are tingling.

"You can't keep doing that, by the way," Agent Belcher says. "You can't just accuse them right to their faces. Patel's going to fire you! He's still your boss!"

He's talking about me and Uncle Anish, of course. Better Uncle Anish than my hair.

Wait. . . . That means Uncle Anish really is a suspect.

And I am too.

"Nah. He can't fire me. That would look too suspicious," Agent Fartz says. "If he fired me, then everyone would think he's covering something up. Anyhow, he's going to be gone soon. You can't disappear a bunch of Zdstrammars because they've been protesting and think that you won't get caught."

"I don't know," Agent Belcher says. "He's supposed to be promoted to head of the FBAI next month."

"Agent Patel might be up for head of the FBAI, but that doesn't mean he's invincible," Agent Fartz says.

The Zdstrammars were protesting? What about?

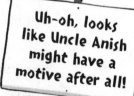

Uh-oh, looks like Uncle Anish might have a motive after all!

"You really think he did it?" Agent Belcher asks.

"What? You think it's a coincidence that that little girl shows up the very same day we have our first MIA in years? Can't be," Agent Fartz says.

I run my fingers through my hair, hoping to loosen some of the knots, but I don't get very far. There's still glue sticking to my scalp. Ouch. This is as bad as the time I got gum stuck in my curls in the first grade. Still better than lice, though. Lice is the worst.

"Here's my theory," Agent Fartz continues. "I think while she was being checked in through security, Agent Patel found a way to smuggle the Zdstrammars out. He gave them what they wanted—more freedom. And now Patel doesn't have to deal with them stirring up trouble with all the other Break Throughs when he becomes FBAI head. That's a win-win." He raises his absurdly bushy brows. "And a motive."

I hear them coming closer to the door. My heart starts thumping in my chest. It's too late to run. My only hope is that they turn to the left and don't notice me. I hold my breath and try to blend with the wall, starfish style.

What if they walk out and catch me here eavesdropping?

Is eavesdropping illegal in Area 51?
Will I go to Area 51 jail?
Is there even an Area 51 jail?

"On the other hand, we don't know enough about the Zdstrammars. Maybe they found a way to signal to their home planet or something," Agent Belcher says.

Last night, Elvis told me that very few Break Throughs have ever successfully returned to their home planets. That they know beforehand that coming to Area 51 is a one-way trip. Apparently most Break Throughs like the idea of settling somewhere new.

"Or maybe I was right the first time and Agent Patel opened the gates and set them free," Agent Fartz says. I see Agent Belcher quickly wipe Fartz's spit out of his eye.

I hold my breath until they turn the corner.

That was a close one.

THIRTEEN

DON'T GET BITTEN BY AN ARTHOGUS!

I WISH ELVIS WERE HERE. THAT'S MY SECOND THOUGHT AS I wind my way through the halls of FBAI looking for the exit.

My first thought is: I'm so glad I'm not in Area 51 jail right now.

Weirdly, though, just as I'm thinking of Elvis, he appears.

"Hey, Sky!" he says, and reaches up for a high five. Huh. Wouldn't have guessed aliens high-five, but then again, I wouldn't have guessed anything I've learned about the universe since coming here. Today Elvis is wearing a T-shirt with a picture of a bowl of ice cream with french fries sticking out. My favorite meal.

Warmth washes through my body. I'm so relieved to see my friend.

"Heard you passed your test! Nice one," Elvis says.

"It was scary," I admit.

"I bet. Agent Patel walkied me to pick you up. He said to tell you he had an emergency and that I should escort you to school." Elvis leads me out of the building to a waiting golf cart. As we walk, I catch him up on the Zdstrammar pee-pee clue.

He jumps into the driver's seat.

Wait, you're allowed to drive?

"Why wouldn't I be allowed to drive?" Elvis asks.

"Because you're twelve!" I say.

"You can too if you want. Here." Elvis shifts over, and I walk around to the other side. I sit behind the wheel.

Holy cannoli.

I've taken shape-shifting aliens in stride, but this—the possibility of *driving*—blows my mind.

"Seriously? Kids are allowed to *drive* here?" I ask, to make extra sure this is not some sort of alien-human misunderstanding. "Is that in the handbook?"

"Page twenty-five. Comes right after the policy

on no contact with the outside world and before the discussion of where to get medical treatment if you're bitten by an Arthogus," Elvis says.

"What's an Arthogus?" I ask.

"You really need to read the handbook, Sky," Elvis says.

Elvis shows me the gas and brake pedals and teaches me how to use the gear shift. It's all simpler than I would have guessed. This makes me wonder what other random things only adults are allowed to do that kids aren't but should be.

Area 51 isn't very populated, so we pass only three other golf carts and a couple of pedestrians on our way. I tell myself it's unlikely I'll kill anyone, human or otherwise. I stay focused on the road, listening as Elvis passes along driving tips. Apparently I keep drifting too close to the other lane, and I also do not need to beep the horn every three seconds. I try not to get distracted by the strange landscape around me.

This place is all desert. Dry and brown and treeless. The only green is fake grass and large umbrellas spaced out to block the sun. Uncle Anish told me that Area 51 has its own power grid, and now I see how it works: solar panels line every single rooftop.

I press harder on the gas pedal to go faster. I want

to feel the wind in my hair. But the golf cart won't push more than twenty-five miles per hour.

Well, I guess that explains why they allow twelve-year-olds to drive here.

"Oh," I say. "So this doesn't go much faster than Autopia at Disneyland."

"I've never been to Disneyland. Is it like Area 51?" Elvis asks.

"Not even a little," I say.

"I wish I could go one day. See the rest of your pretty Earth," Elvis says.

"Do you think that's what happened with the Zdstrammars? I overheard Agent Fartz say they were protesting and he thinks Uncle Anish let them go so they'd stop making trouble." A puff of smoke or cloud—but my instinct tells me it's more solid some-how, not smoke or cloud at all—moves into the road. An alien, of course. I beep the horn, and the smoke/cloud thingy forms a distinct exclamation point.

"Sorry, Sylvie!" Elvis yells out the side of the golf

SYLVIE, apparently

cart, and then says to me, "You are supposed to stop at crosswalks."

"Oops! Sorry!" I slam on the brakes.

"Don't worry. Sylvie's cool. She's from Gasland, which is only two solar systems away. Anyway, that's interesting about Agent Fartz. I overheard my parents talking this morning about how they're worried that Agent Patel won't get his promotion unless the Zdstrammars turn up," Elvis says. "We really have to do something."

I catch my own image in the rearview mirror. This thing may only go about twenty-five miles per hour, but I'm *driving*. I survived my first lie detector test, and I'm on my way to start at a new school full of aliens, some that are made of shape-shifting smoke.

Surely I can team up with my new alien best friend and attempt to solve a national emergency.

"You're right," I say. "We need to get to the bottom of it."

"The top of it too," Elvis says.

FOURTEEN

FIRST DAY OF SCHOOL

BY THE TIME WE GET TO SCHOOL, ELVIS AND I HAVE A PLAN.
Well, sort of. Neither of us has ever done any sort of
real-life sleuthing, beyond my general nosiness. Our
only experience involves having read mystery novels and, in my case, having watched a whole lot of
Scooby-Doo.

ELVIS AND SKY'S PLAN TO
FIND THE ZDSTRAMMMARS:

Step 1. SNOOP.
Step 2. Ummm . . .

Oh well. Our plan will have to wait till two
o'clock anyway. Elvis says we need to get to homeroom before the first bell.

Area 51 Middle School looks nothing like the school I went to in California. Yawn Middle was one big brown building set on a hill. From social studies class I could make out a rectangle of ocean from the window.

Here, strangely, school is hot pink.

"Not all the Break Throughs can see the full range of colors," Elvis says, answering my question before I've even asked it as we pull into a parking lot filled with golf carts. I notice each has a license plate with a name on it. Ours reads *Elvis*. That will make it easier for us to find it later. "But for whatever reason, everyone here seems to able to make out fluorescents."

Walking into the Area 51 school is the most bizarre experience of my life, which is saying a lot, considering the past few days I've had. I know it's rude to stare, and yet how can I not?

"Move it, new kid. Late for math," someone says as they push past me.

"Sky," I yell once I've found my voice. "My name is Sky." The doughy green alien with sixteen eyes turns and examines me with all sixteen eyeballs. Then, unexpectedly, in the center of its belly, a circle that was glowing red turns into a glowing peace sign.

"I'm Marty," it says. "Sorry!"

"Coming through," something—someone?—says, and though I don't see anyone or anything, I feel a cold breeze pass through my body.

"That was Xavier, though we call him Chill," Elvis says.

"Ew," I say.

"I heard that!" Chill calls back, and I'm about to respond, when four aliens that look like Picasso's cubist paintings come to life—all hard shapes organized in an asymmetrical mixed-up human form—pass by, chattering excitedly.

"I heard they found a hole in the west gate and slid through," says a girl who has one eye in the center of her forehead and another in her chin. "I bet they went to Vegas."

"No way," her friend says. "I think this is some sort of publicity stunt to get people to pay attention to their 'cause.'" She makes air quotes with her fingers, which are both attached to her left hip.

"I heard they found a way to beam themselves back to their planet. I'm sooo jealous." This comes from a girl walking on her hands, her giant pouty balloon lips in the middle of her stomach. "I miss home."

"Oh my snoogles, Elvis, is this the new girl?" the forehead-eye girl says, and the group stops and stares at me. I'm not sure where to look, since their eyes are everywhere.

"Hi, I'm Sky," I say, deciding to try the outgoing, friendly route at this school. Back at Yawn Middle, I always felt awkward and out of place.

Here, it's hard to feel awkward and out of place when each alien you pass is weirder than the last.

YAWN MIDDLE   **AREA 51 MIDDLE**

The girls all hold their hands up in peace signs, and this time, without hesitation, I flash a peace sign right back. Maybe Area 51 Middle won't be so bad after all.

· · · FIFTEEN · · ·
FIRST-DAY JITTERS

MY TEACHER, MS. MOLERATTY, IS HUMAN, THOUGH SHE DOES
look a lot like an opossum. She has two long teeth
that reach over her bottom lip, and small brown eyes
set too close together. Spike would love her, since he
feels comfortable with anything rodent-like.

The subjects covered at Area 51 Middle School are a little different than at Yawn. No straight-up math, science, and social studies here.

8:00–8:30	Homeroom/Attendance/Vitals
8:30–9:30	Identifying Flying Objects
9:30–10:30	Climate Change: How to Unchange It
10:30–11:30	Our Cosmic Neighbors and Understanding Our Biosphere
11:30–1:00	Lunch/Break
1:00–1:30	Human Evolution: Why So Slow?
1:30–2:00	Foreign Languages: Zdstrammarese, Inkblit, Peeyou

"Vitals!" Ms. Moleratty calls, and the whole class lines up in the center aisle of the classroom. She has a small laser that she uses to beam light at each student, which then spits out a label with numbers and letters that she affixes to a book on her desk.

"What's that?" I whisper to Elvis, because I'm not sure I like the idea of being shot with a laser after my morning of electrodes. There sure is a lot of poking and prodding in Area 51.

"She's taking vitals," Elvis says, and shrugs. "No

big deal. Records neuron firing levels, central processing center functioning, you know, the usual."

"Right," I mutter. "The usual."

When it's my turn, Ms. Moleratty smiles her opossum-y smile at me.

"Sky Patel-Baum! I've been looking forward to meeting you," she says.

"Are you nervous?" Ms. Moleratty asks me.

Is there anything more nervous-making than someone asking if you are nervous?

No.

No, there is not.

I feel wet under my armpits. This might be worse than the lie detector, because there is a room full of people (people? creatures?) looking at me.

"A little," I admit. "First-day jitters."

"Don't worry. We'll take good care of you here," Ms. Moleratty says, and then licks her opossum-y lips with her opossum-y tongue. I scratch my scalp, still itchy from the glue they used to attach the electrodes. "Everyone, meet Sky Patel-Baum," she announces to the class.

All eyes (and there are lots of them—I saw one Break Through with at least thirty) turn to me. The ones with mouths look like they are smiling. I put up two fingers in a peace sign, and the peace sign gets returned to me in a bunch of different ways. Fingers, glowing bellies, entire bodies morphed into the shape, and in one case a puff of smoke that looks like skywriting.

"Fast learner," Ms. Moleratty says approvingly.

··· SIXTEEN ···
COINCIDENCES

THE DAY MOVES QUICKLY. EVERYONE IS WAY FRIENDLIER than at my old school. Elvis saves me a seat at lunch, so I'm spared that awful first-day *Where do I sit?* feeling. We share a table with a variety of Break Throughs, and even though I'm still curious, it's becoming way easier not to stare. A boy from our class who I'm 99 percent sure is human asks if he can join us.

"Of course," I say, and that same time, Elvis says, "Our table is already crowded, Zane." This seems out of character for Elvis, but I'm too excited about the idea of making new friends.

"We can make room," I offer, and I elbow Elvis to move over.

Zane is white and has brown curly hair and blue eyes. He looks exactly like all the boys at Yawn Middle who never once bothered to talk to me. Except

LUNCH AT YAWN MIDDLE

LUNCH IN AREA 51

he's more muscular. He reminds me of a kid version of a WWE wrestler.

"I know this place can feel weird at first, but you'll get used to it," Zane says.

"Yeah," I say, though I think I'd put it a different way. For the first time in my life, I don't feel like the weird one. To be honest, it's kinda great.

"What's it like being Agent Patel's niece? That dude is serious," Zane says.

"Um." I look at Elvis, but he just shrugs, like *you're the one who invited him to sit down.* "It's cool. I mean, we only recently met, so . . ."

"He's like super important around here. He's my stepdad's boss," Zane says. I'd wonder who his step-dad is, but I know like four people in 51, so I don't bother asking.

"Oh."

"Though probably not for much longer," he says, all casual as he lifts a french fry to his mouth. "Everyone knows that your uncle did something to those Zdstrammars. And he's going to get fired."

"Um. No. That's not true," I say. My grandma taught me to always defend our family. Up until now, that only meant defending her, and she never really needed defending, but still.

SKY: Defender of Family and Freedom! Brave and strong!

ZANE: My new nemesis, my sworn enemy!

Scared the pee-pee out of him!

"Come to think of it, it's so weird that they went missing at the same time you showed up," Zane says.

I do not like this kid.

"Are you implying that I had something to do with the Zdstrammars' disappearance?" I'm mad now. Here I was enjoying myself, thinking that this place might be different from Yawn Middle. I stand up without thinking. I feel Elvis behind me; his hand rests lightly on my shoulder. He doesn't say anything, but I hear him anyway: *I got your back.*

"Not implying. I'm saying it to your face. I have my eyes on you, Sky Patel-Baum," Zane says.

I look at my plate for something to defend myself with. Who am I kidding? These french fries would make for lousy weapons.

OTHER FOODS NOT CURRENTLY AVAILABLE TO ME THAT WOULD MAKE A BETTER WEAPON!

Baguette
Cucumber
Banana peel (for slipping)
Sack of potatoes
Hot sauce!

"How dare you?" I ask, but it's not really a question. Instead, it sounds threatening. Good.

"The Zs went missing at the same second you got here. My stepdad always says there's no such thing as a coincidence," Zane says. "I think you and your uncle had something to do with it."

"Leave her alone, Zane," Elvis says.

"Fine," he says, and picks up his lunch tray—which

is when I realize, of course! A lunch tray would be the perfect weapon. One knock on the head and *kapow!* Zane would be out cold. But I don't attack him. I may have a detailed imagination, but I'm pretty peaceful in real life.

Zane walks away, not a scratch on him.

For the rest of the school day his words echo in my ear: *There's no such thing as a coincidence.*

seventeen

CHECKING OUT THE WEST GATE

"WHAT IF WE ASSUME THERE'S A CONNECTION BETWEEN ME coming here and the Zdstrammars going missing?" I ask Elvis that evening. We are currently at the west gate, the westernmost border of Area 51, to see if we can find any holes that the aliens might have slipped through or any other clues. The thing is, the west gate isn't a gate: it's a giant clear wall with barbed wire on top. I hate it upon sight, even if I can't see very much since it's seven p.m. and already dark.

There are cones set out in a line for about a quarter of a mile to the east. I wonder if they mark the Zdstrammar urine trail. Like the bread crumbs Hansel and Gretel leave behind. Except grosser.

Note to self: The Zdstrammars were likely taken to the east, not through the wall.

"So you're thinking your uncle had something to do with this after all?" Elvis asks. He pats down the wall in big side-to-side swooshes, as if he is cleaning it.

"No. Not necessarily. There just might be a connection, is all I'm saying." Elvis stops moving for a minute to think this idea over. I've noticed he does that—goes still when he's thinking. I want to ask if this is an Elvis thing or a trait of his species, but it feels like a rude question, even for me.

"That's true. Someone could have used you as either a cover or to point the finger at Agent Patel," Elvis says.

"Or both," I say. I place my hand on the wall, and it's cold as ice. I don't like that it's an optical illusion. From a distance it seems you can walk right on through to the other side, and it would be easy to forget it exists.

But walls lock you in as much as they keep other people out.

Elvis says that everyone at Area 51 is happy to live here, that they've all made the choice to come and knew they wouldn't get to live freely beyond these borders. But I really wish Elvis could see Disneyland one day.

"Ew, what's this?" I ask. My hands are somehow covered in a clear, mucus-like substance from touching the wall.

"Looks like it's from a Sanitizoria" Elvis says calmly.

"Excuse me!" I exclaim, trying to shake the liquid off. "WHAT?!"

"Don't worry. It's just hand sanitizer! The Sanitizoria come from a planet that is surrounded by rings of disinfectant. They excrete sanitizer. It's actually super handy. One less thing Area 51 has to import," Elvis says. I sniff the gel. He's right. I take a deep breath and rub my hands together, trying to wrap my brain around the fact that an alien excretion can actually be cleansing.

"But what's it doing on the wall?" I ask.

"No idea," Elvis says.

FAMILY NAME: Sanitizoria

DEFINING CHARACTERISTICS: Extremely weak immune systems. Excrete sanitizer to ensure a germ-free environment.

LIFE SPAN: 45 Earth-years

POPULATION IN AREA 51: 85

HOSTILE OR FRIENDLY: Friendly

I hear a police siren, and all of a sudden a golf cart—one going way more than twenty-five miles per hour—pulls up alongside us. Two uniformed officers get out and shine flashlights in our faces, the second time today that's happened to me.

I also start to sweat. Third time today for that.

Is what we are doing illegal? I really need to read that stupid handbook.

WEST GATE

"Identify yourselves," the first police officer says. She is a short, compact woman with loose, long, glamorous hair that doesn't match her job. Aren't police officers required to wear ponytails? Or hairnets, like lunch ladies?

I see a flash of something out of the corner of my eye and notice my security level hologram has appeared next to me. I've gone up several digits. I'm now a six.

"Elvis Galzoria, ma'am. We're working on a school project about light refraction. Thought the west gate would be perfect to test wave redirection."

"Elvis! Sorry didn't recognize you at first. You look like my ex-husband today, but in the early days, before he grew that silly mustache. It's Officer Glamcop. Tell your mom I say hi! We missed her at poker last week." Officer Glamcop lowers her flashlight so we can see her face. She's older than I would have guessed. About Uncle Anish's age.

She's smiling at us, which is a relief. Elvis whispers to me, "Glamcop is head of the 51 police department."

Officer Glamcop's partner, who stands next to her, is not smiling. He squints at us. He has a tattoo that stretches from his cheek down to his neck. I squint at it. It's some sort of terrifying killer octopus.

He looks like the kind of person who *could* somehow turn a delicious french fry into a weapon.

"Light refraction? Seriously? What are you guys really doing out here?" he asks. I'm frozen with fear. I don't like to lie under normal circumstances. And though I've never actually lied to a police officer, I have a feeling I would enjoy that even less.

"Umm," I say, kicking the dirt.

"Hi, Officer Roidrage! Nice to see you again, sir," Elvis says finally, his voice unnaturally high and overly friendly.

"Elvis!" the officer says angrily.

"Fine. We were looking for a break in the wall," Elvis says, and shrugs.

"You're looking for the Zdstrammars," Officer Roidrage says.

"Yup," Elvis says. "But light refraction is an interesting concept too."

"We heard that rumor. No way the Zdstrammars found a hole. This wall is impenetrable. A few months ago, Agent Belcher drove his golf cart at full speed into it by mistake and the thing didn't even crack a little," Officer Glamcop says. "You must be Sky Patel-Baum. Nice to meet you. Big fan of your uncle's."

I smile back at her, then stop when I see Officer Roidrage's glare. "Get home and quit playing kid detectives, you two." He points the flashlight in our faces one last time as a warning, and somehow, it feels threatening. "If I catch you out here again, we'll take you in."

"They're only kids," Officer Glamcop says.

"He's not a kid, Margaret. He's a Break Through," Officer Roidrage says, and the bite in his voice makes me shiver.

"We're leaving now. Promise," Elvis says, and I follow him back to our golf cart. He drives this time, and when I look at his hands on the steering wheel, I notice they're shaking.

EIGHTEEN

HOME IS WHERE THE MAC 'N' CHEESE IS

"HOW WAS YOUR DAY?" UNCLE ANISH ASKS WHEN I GET home. Huh. This is the first time I've thought of his house that way. As "home."

"Weird," I say. "But not totally bad–weird. Ups and downs."

"Sounds about right around here," Uncle Anish says, getting up from the couch. Spike is on his shoulder. Looks like they've become fast friends. "You hungry? I made dinner." We sit at the small dining table, and he heaps piles of macaroni and cheese onto my plate. The good stuff. From the box. Grandma only let me eat the homemade kind. She said the orange stuff isn't real cheese. *Remember this, Sky: if it's fluorescent, it's not food.* I wonder if that rule also applies to school, and what she would say if she saw that Area 51 Middle is fluorescent pink.

I miss my grandmother, though I don't miss her macaroni and cheese. She always snuck in spinach, like I wouldn't notice the random green bits.

Of course she noticed the random green bits.

WHAT I IMAGINE GRANDMA DOING RIGHT THIS SECOND

All by myself . . .

KARAOKE NIGHT

ALL BY MYSELF . . .

My go-to karaoke song: "Baby Shark"

"So I heard about your little run-in with the law," Uncle Anish says.

"They told you?" I ask.

"Yup. Area 51 is like a small town that way. Everyone knows everyone else's business," he says.

"Are you mad?" I ask.

"Nah. I understand. I admire your curiosity. Maybe when you're older you'll join the FBAI," he says. I've never been one of those kids who feels comfortable when grown-ups ask what they want to be when they grow up; I always shrug.

What do kid orphans with pet hedgehogs grow up to be?

I have no idea.

Adult orphans with pet hedgehogs, maybe?

But now, for just a minute, I imagine becoming an adult and going to that enormous FBAI building every day and studying Break Throughs. Keeping the secrets of the universe safe. It would be my job and my duty to protect the Break Throughs like Elvis. I can almost picture it, though if I ever get the chance to be in Uncle Anish's position I think I'll find a safe way to take down the walls.

Protector of the Universe!

SPIKE: Protector of the Pizza!

"But please, you have to stop investigating. I'm in a spot of trouble, and the last thing I want is for you to get caught up in it," Uncle Anish says.

"Because some people think you let the Zdstrammars go. Or that maybe I did," I say, and Uncle Anish flinches.

"I mean, kind of? Just so you know, I didn't, of course. The Zdstrammars are like family to me. I golf with Blobby every Sunday. I'm worried sick about him," he says.

"What do you think happened?" I ask.

"I'm trying to figure that out. But please let it be. This is dangerous. For real. You're lucky Officer Glamcop was with Officer Roidrage when they found you. I don't know what would have happened if Officer Roidrage had been alone," Uncle Anish says, and I shiver as I remember Officer Roidrage's octopus tattoo, the tentacles etched into the skin around his neck. "I don't have authority over the police force. The FBAI's job is to serve and protect the Break Throughs. Area 51 police enforce 51's laws. Totally different sectors, though we work together."

"What could have happened?" I ask.

"Put it this way: Officer Roidrage is *not* Team Patel," Uncle Anish says.

"Or Team Elvis. You should have seen the way he stared at him. It was a little scary," I admit. I shovel macaroni into my mouth, enjoying the fact that I don't have to pick out green bits. I ignore the clawing in the pit of my stomach as I think about the detail on that tattoo—the finely drawn suckers, which looked like they could suffocate someone.

"What do you see when you look at Elvis?" Uncle Anish asks me.

I shrug. "Just a kid. And he always wears shirts with a picture of something I love on them. It's weird."

"Huh. That's interesting. I knew you two were meant to be friends. You know who Officer Roidrage sees when he looks at Elvis?"

"Who?"

"The kid who bullied him in elementary school, but all grown up. It's a strange phenomenon. We've figured out that with the Galzoria, your perception is linked to how they make you feel. It's not about them so much as it is about you. You're fully comfortable with Elvis, as you should be. That kid's the best. But for whatever reason, Officer Roidrage feels threatened by him," Uncle Anish says.

"Really?" I ask. I can't imagine feeling afraid of Elvis, though that could be because when I look at him, it's like looking at a scrapbook of my favorite things. He's as harmless as I feel in real life.

"Officer Roidrage has a problem with Break Throughs generally. Thinks we give them too much freedom. He was so angry when a bunch of Zs got together recently to protest for permission to occasionally leave the base. If Roidrage had his way . . . You know what? Never mind." Uncle Anish shakes his head, as if to get rid of the thought. I feel cold again. "Just stay out of trouble, please. Do you promise?"

"I need you to do this for me, Sky."

"Question for you: where was Officer Roidrage on the day the Zdstrammars went missing?" I ask. I'm starting to draw up a list of suspects in my mind, and Officer Roidrage is now at the top of it.

"He was on duty at the Area 51 police station, on shift until four. He has an airtight alibi," Uncle Anish says, and frowns.

· · · NINETEEN · · ·

NOT A STARBUCKS IN SIGHT

THE NEXT DAY AFTER SCHOOL, ELVIS AND I DECIDE TO TAKE Spike and Pickles for a walk. Well, Pickles, at least. Spike is more a ride-on-my-shoulder kind of guy, though this time he decides to sit on Pickles like he's a horse.

The walk is, of course, our cover story. We're really still on our mission to investigate.

It's too dangerous to head back to FBAI headquarters right now— I'm sure if anyone sees us they'll report back to Uncle Anish—so we decide to go across town to a café that Elvis says is popular with Zdstrammars. We want to find out if there's any chance the Zs tried to leave the base.

Giddyup, pardner!

Maybe this wasn't a kidnapping at all. Maybe it was an escape mission.

"Is it a Starbucks?" I ask, and my mouth waters as I think about a Frappuccino. I may not miss Grandma's mac 'n' cheese, but I do miss a ton of other food and drinks from my old life. Grandma and I used to go to Starbucks after school on Fridays, and I'd always drink too much sugar and caffeine while Grandma sipped her tea. Afterward we'd go to the beach and build sandcastles.

Grandma always used to say *You are never too old to build sandcastles.* I hope that's true. Though come to think of it, I doubt I'll ever see a beach again: Area 51 is landlocked.

THINGS I MISS FROM MY OLD LIFE:

I miss trees. And Grandma's toilet paper. What? You think hedgehogs don't have to wipe?

Grandma
Frappuccinos
Grandma's toilet paper
(What? It's softer than Uncle Anish's!)
Sandcastles
Tacos
The Internet
Yawn Middle
(ha ha, just kidding!)

"What's a Starbucks?" Elvis asks.

"Never mind," I say, wondering what coffee shops look like in Area 51. So far I haven't seen any actual stores. Is there an Area 51 Target? Probably not.

"That's the library," Elvis says, and points to a building that looks like a medieval castle but is fluorescent lime-green. It's huge and towering and way too bright.

Oooh, I cannot even imagine all the information the library here must hold. Secrets not just about our world but about the entire universe! It must be bursting with them!

I'm definitely looking at it longingly, because Elvis says, "I can show it to you another time, but they don't allow dogs. Or, I assume, hedgehogs."

"Is there a supermarket here? Also, where do people buy clothes?" I ask.

"There's a commissary. They'll retinal-scan you upon entry and then you can take home any food you need. All clothes come from the thrift center. Everything is vintage," Elvis says. "My parents mostly stick to their FBAI uniforms. My mom says it's better than wearing a pink Juicy Couture sweatsuit from the nineties. Apparently there's a large surplus of those."

Well, that explains all the strange styles at school. I look down at my faded jeans and T-shirt. Randomly, I fit in here.

"Once a year we have a supply drop from a helicopter. Most of what is provided comes from GOs—government outsiders—who know the truth about Area 51 and shop local thrift stores to provide clothing and other supplies for us. We always have a party that day. I don't do clothes, but I do love the chocolate drop," Elvis says.

I reach out and touch the striped collared T-shirt Elvis appears to be wearing. It has no image on it. Instead, the T-shirt is just like the one my dad is wearing in the only photograph I have of him. Elvis is solid, and I have all sorts of questions about his solidity. Is that my perception? Does he morph to fit my image of him?

THE ONE PICTURE I HAVE OF MY PARENTS:

This picture makes me almost as happy as PIZZA!

"Can anyone see you as you naturally are? Like your real form?" I ask.

"I mean, other Galzoria do, of course. But not humans or the other non-Galzorian Break Throughs."

"Does that make you sad? That I can't see you?" I ask.

"Not really. In some ways, this is more truthful, don't you think? How you see me is based on our connection. Seems like a better system than the way your people do it. With arbitrary classifications of attractiveness."

"Huh," I say, because sometimes it's hard to keep up with Elvis.

"Come on, let me introduce you to the Zdstrammars. They have the largest population of Break Throughs in 51 because they were the first settlers here and they don't have much trouble adjusting to Earth's atmospheric pressure. They like to stick together, though. Literally." He points across the street.

"Cool," I say, and we run across the street, Pickles and Spike leading the way.

TWENTY

TARGET ON MY BACK

TURNS OUT THE ZOSTRAMMARS ARE SUPER CHATTY AND loud. I don't know where they are talking from—as far as I can tell they have no mouths—but they sure have a lot to say. Their voices are squeaky and high-pitched, and they echo. Echo. Echo.

We sit at an outdoor café, but it doesn't look like anyone is drinking coffee, likely because of the whole, you know, no-mouth issue.

"I miss them so much-much-much," says one, who I think based on their size and whine must be a toddler in human years.

"Yeah, we do too, Snugglebug-bug-bug," says another. She is fused to the little one in multiple places, so I assume they are mother and child. I feel a pang of jealousy.

"Thanks for talking to us about this. I know it's hard," Elvis says, holding his fingers up in a peace sign.

"We don't know what happened. If that's why you're here-here-here," says another Zdstrammar, who is slightly separate from the group.

Elvis whispers in my ear, "Froth, their leader."

"We just want to help," I say.

"And save your uncle's buttocks-tocks-tocks," Froth says.

"Not just his buttocks. The rest of him also. Like his arms and legs and head," Elvis adds.

"I think they get it," I whisper to Elvis.

"Here's what we know: you came, and at the exact same time, three of our brothers and sisters went missing. You do the math-math-math," Froth says.

I like math! But calculus is hard-hard-hard.

Pizza slices are a great way to learn fractions. This is 1/8TH of a pizza.

The other 7/8THS are going in my belly!

"We heard there were protests recently?" Elvis asks, as if we are just chitchatting. Do they allow Break Throughs to join the FBAI? I hope so, because Elvis would make a fantastic officer when he's old enough in Earth-years. Maybe we could be partners!

"No one wanted to leave, if that's what you're asking-ing-ing," Froth says, though she starts to get choked up. "It hadn't gotten that bad. Pop was happy-py-py."

"Pop?" I ask.

"My wife. She's one of the missing. We had grumbles about Area 51, sure. Who doesn't? Not a fan of the recent petty crime especially. We just wanted the occasional privilege to step off base. To come and go as we please. So we made an appeal through the FBAI and the BTWC with a petition. No big deal-deal-deal," Froth says, while Elvis translates into my ear: "BTWC is the Break Through Wellness Committee."

"What did the FBAI and the BTWC say?" I ask.

"Don't know yet. We're still waiting to hear-hear-hear," she says. "Please keep that hedgehog away from us!"

"Don't worry. He won't hurt you. Tell us about the day the other Zs disappeared," I say, and take from my back pocket a little notebook I found in one of Uncle Anish's kitchen drawers.

I like the notebook. It makes me feel official.

"Totally normal day besides your arrival. Pop, Blobby, and Foam were all on patrol at the west gate like every Friday. Officer Roidrage saw them clock in at the 51 police station for their shift, so we know they disappeared after that. They didn't report back after their shift, which ended at three-ee-ee," Froth says.

"On patrol?" I ask.

"They were on security detail. We all have jobs, of course. This is a community-tee-tee," Froth says.

"It's also because your kind are such bad secret keepers," the little one they call Snugglebug says. I look to her mom to explain.

"The FBAI likes to keep the human population low at Area 51 because they've had problems in the past with humans escaping the base and telling the rest of the world about us. Because your population is relatively small, they need to rely on Break Throughs to keep this place safe-safe-safe," she says.

"That's why it's such a big deal that you came here. People generally don't get to just move to Area 51-51-51," Froth says. "They say that Agent Patel was smart enough to negotiate your arrival when he first signed up eleven years ago-go-go."

"Really?" I ask. This is new information. I think about all those *Turn back now!!!* signs I saw.

"Yup. Agent Patel got special permission from the big bosses in Washington when he first joined up, and I heard that some of the other agents were super angry because they never thought to do the same when they first moved. They've been petitioning for years to get their families here with no luck. You should be careful-ful-ful," Froth says.

Somehow, the echo makes this sound even more ominous.

"Why?" I ask.

"Because you obviously have a target on your back-back-back."

SPOILER ALERT:
Froth did not mean it literally.

· · · TWENTY-ONE · · ·

WHERE ARE THE TACOS?

ELVIS INVITES ME OVER FOR DINNER, WHICH IS HOW I FIND myself eating spaghetti and meatballs next door with Lauren and Michael. Spike is invited too, and Michael sets out a plate of radishes for him so he can perch right on the table. When Pickles sees this, he growls.

"Pickles takes his food on the floor," Lauren says apologetically while patting his head. "Otherwise he'd clear all of our plates."

"It's true," Elvis says. "We tried it once as an experiment. Not only did he eat everything, but he knocked over Mom's favorite vase."

"Poor Pickles," I say.

"Poor Mom," Lauren says, and laughs. "I loved that vase."

Pickles barks.

"Don't worry. I know you're sorry," Lauren says, as if it is perfectly normal to have a conversation with a dog. Then I remember she's also mom to the alien who has become my new best friend, so maybe I'm no longer someone who should think about things in terms of "perfectly normal."

"So how long have you lived here?" I ask. Since I've learned it's rare for someone like me to be allowed to move to Area 51, I'm curious how everyone else got here. I can't stop thinking about how Uncle Anish had to convince the government to let me come live with him. I always thought Grandma was forcing him to take me in. That he didn't have any choice in the matter.

Is it possible he *wanted* me to come live with him?

"I'm a legacy," Michael says proudly. "Which means I was born on base. Lauren came at around your age, when her mom transferred from the FBI to the FBAI."

"My dad was FBI too," Lauren says, "and after he died, they thought my mother might be a good candidate for Area 51. She didn't have much family to help out with me where we were stationed in Washington, DC, and everything here in Area 51 is about community. Lots of childcare. Also, people without many family ties are better at keeping quiet. She moved here and never looked back."

"I'll take you to meet my grandma tomorrow if

you want. She's the best. She runs this whole place," Elvis says proudly, and I feel a pang realizing that I'll never be able to introduce Elvis to my grandmother. They would like each other.

"We invited my mom tonight, but she's been busy working with your uncle to find the Zdstrammars," Lauren says.

"She lives on the north side of the base. She likes it better over there because she can see real trees over the border from her backyard. That's what she misses most from her old life," Michael says.

"What do you miss most?" Elvis asks me.

"My grandma," I say. "And tacos. And a bunch of other things."

"We have tacos here. We'll get you some," Lauren says. Pickles barks a few times and then circles the table. He stops first at Elvis, then Elvis's mom and dad, and finally me, and we each offer him a meatball from our hands. Not a taco, but almost as good because it also tastes like home.

Pickles barks one last time. I'm pretty sure he's saying thank you.

· · · TWENTY-TWO · · ·

SOME THINGS DON'T CHANGE

A FEW WEEKS LATER, I'VE GOTTEN USED TO MS. MOLERATTY taking my vitals during homeroom. And sitting in a classroom full of aliens. Also the fluorescent pink walls. The only thing I haven't gotten used to is Zane, who has decided it's his new mission in life to annoy me.

Though, in all fairness, it seems like it's his mission in life to annoy everyone.

In first period, Identifying Flying Objects, Zane sits behind me and kicks my chair so hard my back rattles. In third period, Our Cosmic Neighbors and Understanding Our Biosphere, he waves his hand in front of his nose when I walk by, as if I smell bad. At lunch, when he "accidentally" flips my lunch tray, Elvis tells me to ignore him. That most bullies need attention the same way humans need oxygen. But in language class, as I struggle to grunt in Inkblit, I finally lose it.

"I don't have a problem," he says innocently. "You do."

"What's that supposed to mean?" I ask. Zane shrugs, like none of this really matters to him. Which is obviously a lie, since he's been targeting me since I got here.

Is this about the Zdstrammars? Surely he must realize by now that I'm just a kid. No way I could have masterminded an alien abduction.

"You know that you're not going to get away with this. Some of us care about what happens here in Area 51," Zane says.

"I'm not getting away with anything. I don't even

know what you're talking about," I say, but we don't get to finish our conversation because Ms. Moleratty hushes us. For the rest of class, I feel Zane behind me, angrily staring at the back of my neck. As if there is a literal target there.

"Zane's a bully. Seriously, don't sweat it," Elvis says after school. We are riding in his golf cart, heading to see his grandma by the north gate, and as the breeze massages my face I start to let the day go. So what if some doofus in school hates me? I dealt with a lot worse back at Yawn Middle.

I shake it off and think about my grandma.

I may not know what happened to the Zdstrammars, but I know I had nothing to do with it. And I'm pretty sure neither did Uncle Anish.

I am brave and strong, I remind myself.

"Think your grandma will have any info for us?" I ask, because so far Elvis and I have not made much progress on our alien hunt. The Zdstrammars said they use pee on their planet to keep from getting lost or to help others track them, which is further evidence that this was a kidnapping, not a voluntary escape. I want to ask his grandma about the Sanitizoria—whether they had any beef with the Zs.

"Maybe. I hope so," Elvis says. "But either way, you guys are going to love each other."

"How do you know?"

"The first time we met, she saw me wearing a T-shirt with a picture of my mom on it. It means something that you see me in a similar way," Elvis says.

"Huh," I say.

"Also, she's super cool. Like you," he says, as if my coolness is an agreed-upon fact. And just like that, I forget all about Zane.

···TWENTY-THREE···

DOG BISCUITS AND MILK

ELVIS'S GRANDMOTHER IS ONE OF THOSE OLD LADIES WHO doesn't look old except for her neck, which is ringed like a tree trunk. When she sees us, she breaks into a giant grin. She opens her arms wide for Elvis to run into a hug.

"Hello, darling! And you must be Sky!" She opens her arms even wider, to make room for me. She's so friendly and warm, I can't help but run to her too. "So happy to finally meet you! Come in! Come in!"

We walk into her house, which looks exactly like Uncle Anish's and Elvis's and presumably every other house in Area 51, though hers is homier somehow. There's a blue knitted blanket along the back of the couch, and framed photographs of the moon on the walls, and a bookshelf full of paperbacks.

"Sorry I couldn't make it to dinner last night.

Official business to attend to. You'll find there's never a dull moment here in 51, Sky," Elvis's grandma says. "Now let me get you some milk and cookies, and then we can properly chat."

We follow her to the kitchen, and she sets out a plate of what look more like dog biscuits than cookies.

Don't eat them. Grandma is a terrible baker!

"I heard that!" Elvis's grandma says, and laughs. "Though to be fair I did crack a tooth on one of these yesterday, so be careful."

"Don't risk it," Elvis whispers. "Seriously."

"So you guys are here to find out what I know about the missing Zdstrammars," she says simply as she sits down with us.

"How'd you guess?" Elvis asks.

"Years of training," she says.

"Wow," I say, impressed.

"Just kidding," she says, and cracks up. "Your uncle told me you two have been snooping around. He also said that he told you to leave it alone."

"He did . . . but . . . ," I say, trying to find an excuse for disobeying him but coming up empty. I feel bad about crossing my fingers and toes on a promise.

"Yeah, he also said that you're a Patel so it was unlikely you'd actually listen to him." I laugh, because maybe Uncle Anish knows me better than I know him. I hope that's true. The idea makes me feel a little less alone in the world.

"Well, sorry to disappoint you, kiddos. I'm just as stumped as you are about the Zs," Elvis's grandma says. "I don't think the timing is a coincidence. We were trying to narrow down who knew exactly when you were coming here, but the truth is anyone who wanted to know could have checked the logs. They are not kept confidential."

"Do they keep track of who looks at them?"

Elvis asks, and his grandmother beams back at him proudly.

"Good thinking, but unfortunately no. And there were lots of people who, I'm sorry to say, were unhappy to hear that you were coming, Sky. It's not personal, of course," she says.

"Right," I say, even though it feels a little personal.

"It's hard to let go of the outside world, so when someone gets to have someone they love move here, that can be tricky, you know? Makes them think about all the people they miss," she says. I think of my own grandmother and how badly I want to write to her and tell her all about my new life. How I wish there were a retirement facility in Area 51 so I could visit her on afternoons like this one and she could give me some of her homemade cookies, which were always delicious. She used to ask me if I could taste the "extra love baked in." I always could.

"Did the Sanitizoria have any issues with the Zdstrammars?" I ask.

"The Sanitizoria?" Elvis grandma looks confused and then thoughtful. "I mean, they did recently put in a complaint about the Zs' noisiness. But I think every species has at some point. The Zs' volume can be . . . irritating."

"Huh," I say.

"I can't stop thinking about people being mad about Sky coming," Elvis says. "Could someone have been so angry that they wanted to get Agent Patel fired?"

"Now, *that's* an excellent question," Elvis's grandma says.

TWENTY-FOUR

POP GO THE ZDSTRAMMARS!

"DID YOU KNOW THE FIRST FLYING SAUCER WAS SIGHTED above Area 51 in 1947?" Elvis asks me. We are in the library, sitting at one of the long tables in the middle of the room, surrounded by open books. We're trying to learn more about the Zdstrammars, since we seem to have hit another dead end. We have no way of knowing who, if anyone, tried to get their family moved to Area 51 and was rejected. Apparently those sorts of requests get sent through some complicated back channel to Elvis's grandmother's boss in Washington, DC.

And though I have my suspicions about the Sanitizoria, I have no idea what to do about them. According to Elvis, there are tons of them in 51. Their population is almost as big as the Zs'.

"Really? Is that how you came here? In a flying saucer?" I ask, and Elvis giggles, and then stops for a minute and looks at me. When he realizes I'm serious, he starts laughing all over again. "What? What's so funny?"

"Flying saucers are very old technology. That's like asking if the last time someone called you they used a telegram," Elvis says. "No, worse. Like if instead of showing me a book, you showed me a cave drawing. Or instead of driving a golf cart, you rode a horse. Or . . ."

"I get the point," I say, smiling now, because his laughter is contagious. "Sorry I'm not up on the latest alien spacecraft. So how did you come here?"

"The FBAI would call it an Unidentified Aerial Phenomenon, or a UAP, even though I guess technically they've been identified. You know how they love their acronyms," Elvis says.

"The simplest way to think of it is like a vacuum. The Galzoria have technology that uses suction to open an entrance to Earth's atmosphere with set coordinates to Area 51. There's another portal in Asia, too, but as

An acronym is a word made up of the first letters of other words. For example, PICKLE: Partner In Crime Kerfuffles Like Eatingpizza.

far as I know there's no communication between the two bases." I try to picture it: Elvis being sucked down from the sky and losing his parents en route. My stomach cramps.

"Is that how all the Break Throughs, you know, broke through? With a vacuum?" I ask.

"Nope. Each species has found its way here from its own planet using their own technology. We've traveled varying distances and come from very different biospheres, so what works for some doesn't work for all. I mean, look at this," Elvis says, and points to a page in the picture book he's reading.

"You see how the Zdstrammars travel in large groups? As I mentioned, they have little trouble with gravitational forces. They don't need sophisticated vacuums." Ugh. I hate when Elvis shows off his cognitive processing speed. I'm barely following.

"What do you think it means that the aliens who went missing were from the largest group? Do you think there's a connection? Like someone thought no one would notice?" I ask.

"No way. We keep very careful track of everyone in Area 51, humans and Break Throughs alike. Not only for population counts, which are important, of course, but for health protocols. Occasionally you humans develop diseases that can hurt us, so we keep careful track of our vitals." Elvis taps the page a few times, lost in thought. "Speaking of keeping track, hand me that other book."

I toss over a more detailed guide to the Zdstrammars, this one written for scientists and not for the Area 51 kindergarteners. Elvis opens the cover and checks inside. Area 51 uses an old-fashioned library system—to take out a book, you have to sign the card. Except for security protocols and drone-delivered pizza, it seems like this place intentionally likes to avoid computers or technology. This must be how it stays off the grid, whatever that actually means.

"Look!" Elvis says, and starts opening the covers to all the books. "They were all recently signed out by the same person. Want to know the last person who was researching the Zdstrammars before they went missing?"

I look where he's pointing.

"No way," I say.

"Yes way," Elvis says.

TWENTY-FIVE

EXTRA CRUNCH IN YOUR LUNCH

ELVIS AND I ARE SITTING AT LUNCH AT SCHOOL TRYING TO come up with a plan for how to approach Zane.

"You mean you want us to just march up to the biggest bully in school and be like, 'Hey, we know you took out a bunch of books from the library about Zdstrammars the week before they went missing and that's super creepy and suspicious. So what's up with that?'" Elvis asks. I decide to ignore his sarcasm. Who knew aliens could even be sarcastic?

"Exactly. What's the worst that can happen?" I ask.

"It's unlikely in this galaxy, but on my home planet we were deeply worried about asteroids," Elvis says.

"I mean, what's the worst that can happen if we talk to Zane?" I eat a french fry off Elvis's plate. Turns out the food at 51 Middle is surprisingly good. You just need to avoid one particular lunch lady, who is from Retinaya, because one of her thousand eyeballs sometimes falls out into your lunch. Elvis accidentally ate one yesterday. He said it tasted like chicken.

But crispier.

"Right. I don't know. Zane could threaten to beat us up," Elvis says.

"Nah. I'm not scared of him," I say, and before I can reach for another fry, Elvis pushes his lunch tray

in front of me for easier access. I'm learning that one of the many perks of having friends is they share. At Yawn Middle, when I didn't eat in the bathroom, I used to eat alone in the library with only Mrs. Reader, the librarian, for company. She liked to talk about books, which was nice, but she never offered me her potato chips.

"I'm scared of him," Elvis says. "He's legit scary. Twelve-year-olds aren't supposed to have muscles."

"Zane's a doofus," I say.

"A doofus who once sat on me for a solid ten minutes. Pretended he couldn't see me. But he saw me. He was mad that I scored higher than he did on our Name the Black Hole test," Elvis says. "If he kidnapped three Zdstrammars, what do you think he'd do with a Galzoria and a human?"

"I have no idea," I say.

"He'll eat us for breakfast," Elvis says. "Chomp, chomp."

We compromise. I am not supposed to accuse Zane outright. Instead, Elvis and I have decided to try a more casual, relaxed route. Circle the question. Try to make peace first. Even though Zane is our number one suspect, I really don't think he's capable of kidnapping us with that lunch lady's 999 eyeballs watching.

"Hey, Zane," I say, walking up to his table, as if we always chat after we eat our sandwiches. As if it's not at all awkward to be talking to the only kid at school who makes me feel like I used to feel at Yawn Middle—weird and unliked and targeted.

"What do you want?" Zane asks.

"I was just wondering . . . I mean . . . you obviously have a problem with me, and so I wanted to . . . um . . . clear the air," I say. I don't ask what I really want to know: *Why did you do it? Why kidnap the Zdstrammars? What's your motive?* Elvis and I racked our brains, or as Elvis calls his, his central processing center, and we came up with nothing.

"Clear the air," he imitates me mockingly. "What, like you're a Peeyou?"

"Peeyous, from the planet Peeyouranus, give off a biosignature scent, which is such a stinky gas that they have to be retrofitted with air-freshener dispensers here," Elvis explains to me.

"So what you're saying is they smell like farts?" I ask.

"Like a bajillion farts after a bajillion humans ate egg salad," Elvis says.

"Got it," I say, then realize we have veered way off topic.

THE TOPIC

Did Zane kidnap the Zs?

Off Topic

I like egg salad, especially on pizza!

"Zane, I think you're mad at me because I got to move here to Area 51. I didn't realize that was such a special privilege, but I'm starting to understand," I say. "And I'm sorry if you were hoping someone close to you could also move—"

"No. I'm mad at you because your uncle kidnapped someone important to me," Zane blurts, and he looks as surprised as we are by what he just said. *Someone important to him?*

When Zane looks up at me, his face is pinched and sad. There are deep blue circles under his eyes.

"Wait, what?" Elvis asks, because I'm too gobsmacked to answer. This is not what we were expecting.

"Blobby! He's been my next-door neighbor since I was born, and yeah, he was a grown-up Zdstrammar, but he was like a dad to me and now he's gone." If I didn't already know that Zane is a mean bully, I'd think he was about to cry. "I go to this ridiculous school where, like, everyone hates me, and both my mom and stepdad work late all the time. Blobby used to watch me after school. It was the only good part of my day. And then *you* came along and now I'm probably never going to see him again."

He points at me, though he's lost some of his anger. His sadness is way bigger than his rage.

"I'm so sorry about your friend, Zane," Elvis says.

"I'm sorry too," I say.

"I don't need your pity. I just want to get Blobby back," Zane says. I look at Elvis and he nods back at me. That's something else I've noticed about having friends—you can sometimes talk without having to say anything out loud.

"We've been working on that. We want the Zdstrammars to come back as much as you do," I say.

"I highly doubt that," Zane says.

"We do. If my uncle is in trouble, that means I'm in trouble, so I really need to figure this out," I say.

"Whatever," Zane says. "I don't care about your uncle."

I try another approach. "Unrelated to my uncle, we also really just want to solve this mystery. I hate when there are questions I can't answer," I say. "Like, why is it considered okay to sneeze in public but not fart?"

Elvis gives me a strange look. Oops. Again I'm veering off track.

"When we were investigating, we discovered that you took out a bunch of books from the library about the Zdstrammars," Elvis says. "The week before Blobby and his crew went missing."

Zane hangs his head, and I think for just a minute that this will turn into one of those moments on television where the bad guy shamefully confesses.

Maybe Blobby was unhappy in Area 51, and Zane helped him escape but now regrets it? Maybe Zane will rip off his face and reveal that he's actually an evil Break Through underneath? A million possibilities go through my mind, none of which are what actually happens.

Instead, Zane bursts into loud, gulping tears.

TWENTY-SIX

READ THE HANDBOOK

"DO YOU BELIEVE HIM?" I ASK ELVIS LATER. WE ARE BACK at my empty house after school, eating Oreos and drinking milk. Pickles and Spike are playing the game where Spike tries to stay on Pickles's back while Pickles tries to shake him off. So far, Pickles is definitely winning.

"Zane's tears looked real," Elvis says.

"Yeah," I say, and surprise myself by feeling sorry for Zane. I know what it's like to be lonely. Zane told us that Blobby's birthday was coming up, so he took out the books to come up with a cool present. He wanted to learn more about the Zdstrammars' home planet because Blobby said he sometimes missed it. "I think I believe him."

"Yeah, I'm pretty sure I do too," Elvis says.

"Which leaves us back at square one. What do we do—" But I don't get to finish my question because

Uncle Anish comes running into the house, a blizzard of activity.

Uncle Anish sounds frantic and frightened. No *hello, how was your day?* Just *where's your passport?*

"Umm, in my duffel bag," I say, which is where Grandma packed it when I first came to 51. I look at Elvis and he looks back at me, eyes wide. *Am I going somewhere?* An icy feeling spreads down my back. I don't want to leave 51, especially not when it's just starting to feel like home. But because he's so frantic,

I run to my bedroom and pull out the ziplock bag that Grandma labeled *Important documents* with a bullet-point list of each item enclosed: passport, birth certificate, social security card. I hand it to Uncle Anish, my gut too tight. *Please don't make me leave.*

"Thanks, kid," Uncle Anish says, snatching the bag and running toward the door. But then he stops, turns back, and gives me a quick hug.

This scares me more than anything else.

"I'm going to be late tonight, so I'll call you guys in a Code 61154," he says.

Uncle Anish sprints out into the night.

"Thanks," I call after him, though I don't think pizza is going to fix anything.

Back in California, I had a cell phone. I wasn't allowed to use it much. Only for texting Grandma. And playing my Spotify playlist. I haven't missed it at all since coming here.

Until now.

All I want to do is text Uncle Anish and ask him

What's going on? Why do you need my passport? What was with the hug? Are we going on an international trip? Am I moving again? Also, did someone Marie Kondo your home or have you never owned much stuff?

I've never actually traveled abroad—Grandma applied for my passport as a *just in case*. I never knew what that *just in case* could be, seeing as we didn't have money for travel. *Just in case* she won the lottery *and* had a sudden urge for us to see Paris?

Now I wonder if that *just in case* was for 51. My passport was checked on arrival. Maybe she also knew that one day I might have to flee.

"Stop stressing. I'm sure it's fine," Elvis says, after collecting the pizza from a drone at the door and then shoveling a slice directly into his mouth. He has a piece of stringy cheese hanging from his lip.

"Nothing is fine! Someone is obviously trying to frame Uncle Anish. And now he needs my passport so we can run away," I say.

"You humans are very good at jumping to conclusions," Elvis says. Pickles and Spike both nod in agreement. "On Galzoria, we don't jump to conclusions. We meander our way there."

"Give me one good explanation for why he needed my passport," I challenge him.

"I don't have one." Elvis shrugs, like it's not a big deal.

"See!" I exclaim.

"Just because I don't have a good explanation doesn't mean there isn't one. Look what happened with Zane. We were one hundred percent convinced he kidnapped the Zdstrammars, even when we couldn't think of a single reason why he'd do it, and then it turned out we couldn't have been more wrong. Also, if you were running away, would Agent Patel have ordered a Code 61154?" Elvis asks.

"What does ordering a pizza have to do with anything?" I ask.

"You obviously haven't read the handbook yet," Elvis says in a disappointed tone.

"This is not in the handbook," I say with a confidence I don't feel.

RULE #9982993, SUBPART B:

In the rare case that you leave the Area 51 base, do not do it with a full stomach.

256

I give Elvis a questioning look.

"It's an important rule," he says.

"Okay, I'll bite—pun fully intended. Why can't you leave the base with a full stomach?" I ask.

"Isn't it obvious?" he asks.

"Nope. Not to me," I say.

"On the rare occasion someone gets permission to leave, they get x-rayed. If they have a full stomach, the screeners can't tell if it's food or a smuggled Break Through. Hence, if a human is allowed off base, no eating beforehand."

"He's joking, right?" I look at Pickles, who wags his tail, which causes Spike to fall to the floor. I look back at Elvis. "You're joking. They think people would eat a Break Through to smuggle them out? That's bananas."

"No one would eat a Peeyou, but with other species it could happen. I mean, look at what happened with the Arthogus," Elvis says.

"What's an Arthogus?" I ask.

"Dude, you really need to read the handbook," Elvis says, shaking his head at me.

· · · TWENTY-SEVEN · · ·
AN UNWELCOME VISITOR

I WAKE TO LOUD BANGING ON THE FRONT DOOR AND JOLT upright. Apparently I fell asleep on the couch in the living room waiting for Uncle Anish. I'm tucked under a blanket that I've never seen before, though it looks like something Grandma might have knitted. Uncle Anish must have come home last night. *Phew.*

Jumping to my feet, I look around. Where *is* Uncle Anish? I peek into the kitchen, but his coffee mug is hanging on the drying rack, his breakfast dishes already washed.

"Uncle Anish?" I whisper-yell. I don't know whether I'm supposed to answer the door. I don't think there's a mail person or mail Break Through in 51, but even if there is, I don't think they'd knock like this. I peek into my uncle's bedroom. The room is empty, the bed made neatly. Uncle Anish is nowhere to be found, and the knocking is growing more insistent.

Maybe I should go into the hatch? No. No way I'm going into that cold basement without Elvis and Pickles. That feels even more terrifying than facing whoever is on the other side of the door. I pick up Spike and let his quills tickle my cheek. He might be small, but he's still comforting.

"Coming!" I call brightly, like I'm not afraid at all. I take a deep breath and look through the peephole: it's Agent Fartz, whose absurdly bushy brows have somehow grown even thicker and longer than the last time I saw him a few weeks ago. I want to ask if he could braid them and then remember that Agent Fartz is not #TeamPatel.

I open the door.

"Where's your uncle?" Agent Fartz says, and walks by me straight into the house. I leave the door a tiny bit open behind him, in case I need to run. Agent Fartz makes me nervous.

"Please come in," I say, even though he's already walked down the hall and checked both bedrooms, and is now leaning against the old television set. I half wonder if he's going to pick it up and throw me down the hatch. I tell myself there's no way he knows the code.

"Where's your uncle?" Agent Fartz asks again.

"I have no idea. My best guess is FBAI

headquarters," I say. I try to send a telepathic message to Elvis that I might be in danger, but as far as I know, aliens—even alien best friends—don't have those sorts of special powers.

"Cute porcupine," Agent Fartz says.

"He's a hedgehog."

When I was growing up, we used to eat hedgehog stew.

"My uncle's not here. I think you should leave," I say. I notice he has a heavy flashlight and something that looks like a weapon attached to his belt. Both make me even more nervous, and I feel sweat gather at the small of my back.

"I have a few questions for you. Might as well ask, since I'm here anyway," Agent Fartz says.

"I answered all your questions during the lie detector test," I say.

"That was for security clearance. I want to know what happened to the Zdstrammars," he says, and I hear the television creak as it moves a little to the left.

"Do you really think I know anything?" I ask.

"I think you know more than you're letting on. I think you coming at the exact moment they went missing isn't a coincidence. I think your uncle wanted to get rid of the Zs so their little protests didn't hurt his chances of getting a promotion. When did you find out you were moving to 51?"

I pause, then decide the truth is on my and Uncle Anish's side.

"I had barely even heard of 51 until I came." I lift Spike off my shoulder and put him on the ground. I don't have to say anything to my hedgehog. We've been friends for long enough that he knows what to do.

"Convenient," Agent Fartz sneers, and menacingly takes a step closer to me.

Hurry, I think. *Spike, hurry!*

"Do you know how long I've been trying to get permission for my brother to be transferred here? Ten years. No luck. Patel puts in a request, and what? You're here in a week. Something doesn't smell right."

A person named Fartz saying something doesn't smell right? I want to laugh, but I'm too scared. Also, my Spidey sense perks up again. This sounds a lot like . . . a motive.

"I'm sorry about your brother," I say, because I am. It *stinks* that other people can't move their families here also.

Ha! I guess you're never too scared for fart puns.

I don't tell him that my uncle negotiated for my eventual arrival years ago, when he first moved here. I feel like that will only make him angrier.

Agent Fartz doesn't acknowledge my words. Instead, he walks around the room, picks up a candlestick, and puts it back down. He's a big guy. If it came to it, I have no doubt he could kill me with that thing.

"I'm just going to take a look around, if you don't mind." He says this in a way that makes it clear he's not really asking for permission.

I knew Elvis's grandmother was respected in 51, but I didn't realize just how much. Agent Fartz is practically bowing.

"It's good to see you," he says. "I was just doing my job, looking for the Zs."

"Get out of here, Fartz," Elvis's grandma says. "Oh, and tell that partner of yours, Belcher, to turn down the music at his house. We've been getting noise complaints all week."

"Will do," he says, pink in the face, and then scrambles out of the house without another word.

"Don't let the door hit you on the way out, you *stinker*," Elvis calls after him.

"He's moving so fast he's *breaking wind*," Elvis's grandma says.

"That's not nice to make him the butt of the joke," I say.

"Smell you later," Elvis says, and we all crack up.

TWENTY-EIGHT

AN UNEXPECTED ALLY

ELVIS'S GRANDMA MUST HAVE A SPECIAL GOLF CART, BECAUSE when she drives us to school, she speeds down the center of the street going at least fifty miles per hour. She doesn't brake for pedestrians or stop signs, just plows on through, expecting everyone to get out of her way. Amazingly, they do.

"She hates Fartz," Elvis says.

"Why?" I ask. Elvis's grandma is speeding so fast, I'm worried I won't be able to keep down the breakfast I grabbed on the way out the door. Which would be a shame, because I stuffed my face with waffles, and waffles are delicious.

Waffles are cool because they are both a noun and a verb!

"Fartz is a bully. If there's one thing that makes my grandma go ballistic, it's bullies. She'll definitely report him for talking to you like that. You're a kid. It's not okay," Elvis says.

Elvis's grandma already gave me a long lecture about never opening Uncle Anish's door to unexpected visitors ever again. Not that it was necessary—I learned my lesson.

I'm still shaken up. I can't stop thinking about the way Fartz handled that candlestick. How easily he could have bashed in my skull had he wanted to.

I might be brave, but I'm not stupid.

"I think Fartz did it. He has a motive," I whisper to Elvis, but before I can continue we've pulled up in front of school. The cart comes to a quick stop, and it screeches as we jerk forward and back. Elvis and I jump out.

"Stay out of trouble, you two," Elvis's grandma says.

"Thanks for the ride. And for saving me back there," I say, but she just waves her hand like she's the queen of England and reverses out of the parking lot, barely glancing in her rearview mirror. The girls who look like Picasso's cubist paintings have to scramble out of the way to avoid getting hit.

"I need to talk to you guys," Zane calls as Elvis and I are about to walk into school. He's waiting for us by the front door. "Privately."

We have a few minutes before the bell, so we go around the back of the building. We're the only ones out here. There's a bench under an umbrella in the shape of a palm tree. The "leaves" are made of solar panels. I can't decide if I think it's cool or sad.

"Sit," Zane says, and I wonder if, for the second time today, I'm about to find myself in a dangerous situation. Could Elvis take down Zane if he came at us? I honestly don't know. All I know is that Zane could snap me like a twig if he wanted to. Maybe when things calm down around here, I'll find out if there's a gym so I can start lifting weights.

Elvis is right, though. It's super weird for a twelve-year-old to have muscles.

Elvis and I sit down side by side. I wonder if he is as freaked out by this morning as I am.

Zane clears his throat, like he's about to start a long lecture.

"So I don't trust you. Either of you. Not even a little," Zane says. "But I don't think I have a choice."

"About what?" I ask. I feel like he accidentally started midspeech.

"I want to work with you," Zane says.

"What?!" Elvis asks.

"Come on! Don't make me say it again. I want to work with you guys. I want to find Blobby. And the rest of the Zdstrammars. I think we should work together," Zane says.

Lots of weird things have happened since I moved to Area 51.

WEIRD THINGS THAT HAVE HAPPENED SINCE I MOVED TO AREA 51:

1. I helped one of the Picasso girls remove a toe that had gotten stuck in her hair.

2. A giant jellyfish cheated off me on my Biosphere test.

3. When I met my first Peeyou, he handed me an airplane barf bag in case I couldn't handle the smell. He was right. I couldn't.

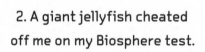

But the fact that Zane, my least favorite person in all of Area 51, wants to team up to solve the mystery of the missing Zdstrammars may be the weirdest.

"Sure," Elvis says at the exact same moment I say "No way."

I shoot Elvis a look.

"What?" he asks.

"I think Elvis and I need a moment to talk about it," I tell Zane.

"What's there to talk about?" Elvis asks, and he looks genuinely confused.

"Elvis!" I say.

"Okay, okay," he says.

"Can we get back to you, Zane?" I ask.

Zane nods and starts to walk away, droopy and sad. I almost feel bad for him and then remember I don't like him. He turns around.

"I'm sorry if I made your first couple of weeks here in 51 harder." My mouth falls open in shock. "Anyhow, no pressure, but the sooner you let me know about working together, the better. I'm afraid we're running out of time." Zane shoots us a peace sign and then turns the corner.

"I don't get it. Why wouldn't we work with Zane?" Elvis asks a few minutes later.

"Maybe because he's the meanest kid in school. Don't you remember the whole sitting-on-you-for-ten-minutes incident? And the fact that he likes to torture me for funsies?" We're definitely going to be late to first period, but suddenly school doesn't feel all that important. I think about the passport that Uncle Anish took, how he was gone this morning before I woke up. The angry look on Agent Fartz's face. Things are moving too quickly. I wonder if it's inevitable that my uncle and I will be banished from Area 51. Or something even worse.

"We haven't gotten all that far on our own. . . . Maybe it will help to have a different perspective," Elvis says.

"But it's *Zane*," I say.

"You humans and your grudges," Elvis says. "True, I used to not like that human, but now that I understand him and why he is the way he is, he's way easier to like. Zane is obviously lonely."

"So?" I know I sound ungenerous. "Didn't you tell me this morning that bullying is not okay?"

"Of course it's not. And if Zane doesn't treat us with respect from now on, we walk away. But I believe that everyone—people and Break Throughs—makes mistakes sometimes. And if they realize that and apologize and try to fix their mistakes, it usually makes sense to forgive them."

I think about the kids at my old school and how Zane reminded me too much of them. I wonder if my anger wasn't only about the way he was treating me.

"You really think we can trust Zane? You believe he had nothing to do with the Zdstrammars going missing? He's not like a double agent or something?" I ask.

"I'm not sure I trust him, but I think it could help to work together. And I don't think he's a double agent. Those tears felt real to me."

"Me too," I grudgingly admit.

"Are you in, then?" Elvis asks. I look up to the palm tree, imagine it harnessing the power of the sun to keep this whole place running. I decide it's definitely cool.

I look at Elvis's shirt and notice that today it has a picture of me. *You are brave and strong,* I hear Grandma say in my mind.

"I'm in," I say.

TWENTY-NINE

GNOMES, GNOMES EVERYWHERE

ZANE, ELVIS, AND I MEET UP AFTER SCHOOL AND HEAD TO Zane's house, because he says that no one will be home. His house looks like Uncle Anish's and Elvis's, except it's painted baby blue. Unlike anywhere else in 51, his lawn is decorated with a shocking number of homemade ceramic gnomes.

"Don't ask," Zane says in a warning tone, when I raise an eyebrow.

"But there are so many," Elvis says, not taking the hint. "Look at that one. He's sunbathing! So cute!"

Ooh, my favorite!

There's a gnome with a pointy red hat and wraparound sunglasses relaxing on a beach chair. Another is reading a book.

"You have to admit, this one is kind of neat," I say, smiling.

"Stop," Zane says.

"It's nice that your house looks different. Seriously," I say. I like the gnomes, and I'm trying hard to be kind to Zane. Maybe this time we can figure out how to be . . . if not friends, exactly, at least partners in crime-solving.

"It's so embarrassing. But my stepdad loves making them. No idea why." We follow Zane into the house, and when we walk inside I gasp.

"How did I not know that?" Elvis asks.

"You know my stepdad?" Zane asks.

"He did my lie detector test. And he scared the spaghetti out of me this morning when he stopped by to see my uncle. But I'm confused: you have different last names," I say. Then I realize my confusion doesn't make any sense. I have two last names, and every time people act confused by that, I think: Dude, what's so confusing about gender equality?

"He's my stepdad. Also, would you choose the name Fartz if you had a choice?"

"No, that name blows," I say, unable to stop myself from making the terrible pun.

"I have my dad's last name, which is pretty much the only thing I have of his. My dad lives in New York. I think," Zane says, looking down and then back up. "He left my mom when I was little. And then we moved here."

"I'm sorry," I say, and he shrugs. "So your stepdad is partners with Agent Belcher, right?"

"Yeah. They don't always get along, though. I mean, to be honest, my stepdad is not the easiest person to get along with," Zane says, and that's when, for the first time today, I think maybe I can trust Zane.

☢ ☢ ☢

"He attacked you?" Zane asks after Elvis and I tell him the whole story of this morning. How Agent

Fartz showed up at my door and waltzed inside and then threatened me.

"No. But it was scary. Like for real, I thought he wanted to kill me," I say.

"No way! My stepdad would never hurt anyone. He won't even let my mom swat a fly. He can be gruff sometimes, sure. And he really thinks your uncle is responsible for what happened. But he'd never hurt you. I promise." We are sitting at a picnic table in Zane's backyard. Zane has put out a bunch of snacks for us all arranged on a pretty platter. Nuts and dried fruit and even cheese with a little special knife in the shape of, yup, a gnome. It's hard to imagine that this version of Zane is the same boy who last week told me I wasn't welcome in 51.

And yet, I'm starting to get it. He truly thought I had something to do with someone he cared about going missing. If someone took Grandma or Elvis, I would go bananas.

"Is that Blobby's house?" Elvis asks, pointing to the right.

"Yup," Zane says, and before I can ask how Elvis knew, I see the Bubble Wrap around the fence, and chairs, and anything pointy. As I've learned, Zdstrammars stay far away from sharp objects for obvious reasons. "I'm worried about him. Zdstrammars are tough emotionally but not physically. If whoever has them isn't careful, they could hurt them."

I don't want to think about that. Instead, I take a bite of a walnut, which reminds me of my grandmother. She used to make me eat nuts before a big test at school. She claimed they were brain food. Thinking of her causes a wave of love and sadness. I'm really starting to like 51, but that doesn't mean I don't miss my old life sometimes.

"Are we a hundred percent sure they didn't just go back to their own planet?" I ask. "Maybe they were homesick. Maybe there's another reason for the pee besides them being kidnapped. Like maybe they were nervous about how'd they'd get back or something."

"No way," Zane says. "Blobby occasionally missed Zdstrammar, but he was happy in 51. He always talked about how lucky I was to grow up here, and how lucky he was that he got chosen by the leaders on his planet to come here. How it was considered a great honor on Zdstrammaroos. He was definitely taken. So let's talk suspects. Who is number one on your list?"

"Umm, I mean, *you* were," Elvis says.

"But now, obviously, you're not," I say.

Zane laughs, and then stops.

"Wait, you're serious? You thought *I* did it?"

"Well, you thought *I* did it. So now we're even," I say, grinning, and I put up a peace sign. He flashes one back.

"What about Fartz?" I ask.

"I'm not saying this because he's my stepdad, but no way. He was at your house this morning trying to get information. He's been very vocal about blaming your uncle. Would he bother to do all that if he was the one who took them?" Zane asks. "It doesn't make sense."

"Or it makes total sense. He did it and wants to make it look like he didn't," I say.

"So Fartz is basically in a *whoever smelt it dealt it* situation," Elvis says, and then we laugh so hard that bits of brain food end up coming out our noses.

THIRTY

PARTNERS IN CRIME

"ARE WE SURE THIS IS A GOOD IDEA?" I ASK. WE HAVE ditched Elvis's family golf cart on the side of the road three blocks from FBAI headquarters, and now we've taken cover behind a side wall near the entrance. The plan is to sneak into the building and look for more evidence that we've missed.

When Zane first proposes sneaking in, I point out that "sneaking in" is just a less illegal-sounding way of saying "breaking in." We're partners in crime-solving, not partners in actual crime.

"Let's vote on it," I say. "All in favor of committing a crime, raise your hand."

It's two to one! Let's do this!

"Okay, here's the plan," Zane says, and his voice goes all secret agent-y. "Sky, you tell security you're here to see your uncle and that your name should be on the appointment list. We'll hide around the corner, and while you keep the guard distracted, we'll slip in and then meet you inside. Got it?"

"Got it," I say, even though I do not got it. When Uncle Anish finds out about this, which he will, he'll probably ground me for life, if he doesn't kill me first.

It would be a shame to have survived my brush with death this morning only to be murdered tonight.

"We'll be fine. I promise," Elvis says. "Just stay away from any Arthogus."

"Wait, what's an Arthogus?" I ask. Elvis giggles.

"I told you to read the handbook!"

☢ ☢ ☢

The security guard at the guest entrance checks her list twice, then squints at me.

"You're not on the list," she says gruffly. She's a large older woman, probably nearing eighty, with a back bent forward like the letter C. I could outrun her if I had to, but I notice that she has a weaponlike object on her belt that I've seen on guards throughout 51. I've been too scared to ask Uncle Anish if it's a gun, but even it's not, it's definitely at least a second cousin twice related to a gun. That's close enough to be scary.

"I should be," I say, in my most innocent little-girl voice. "He's my uncle."

"Wait, you're Sky?" the security guard asks, and her entire face brightens. She smiles widely at me, showing off her white gleaming dentures. "I can't believe I didn't recognize you. Your uncle has talked about you for years. I heard that you are the best egg!"

"Um, thank you," I say.

"Can I hug you? Do you mind? We don't get many newcomers here, not to mention human kid ones. You're a sight for these sore eyes."

"Sure," I say, and the woman steps out of the booth, throws her arms around me, and rocks me side to side. The perfect opportunity. My head is buried in her large bosom, so I don't see Elvis and

Zane run by, but I sense it with a slight prickling in my back.

"Now go on in. Your uncle's office is on the third floor, second door on the left. Welcome to 51, dear!" the security guard says.

"That was too easy," I say, when I meet up with Elvis and Zane around the corner from the sweetest security guard in the world. I make a mental note to bring her homemade cookies tomorrow as a thank-you. I feel a tiny bit guilty taking advantage of her kindness, especially because she reminded me of my grandma.

"Don't say that. You'll jinx us," Zane says, and Elvis giggles. "What's so funny?"

"You humans and your need to believe in the concept of a controllable fate. It's sort of adorable," Elvis says, shaking his head. I don't have time to ask Elvis what Galzoria believe in, because we hear some agents rounding the corner.

"Come on," I say, leading Elvis and Zane to a tiny alcove with a drinking fountain. We hide behind it, bending our bodies like pretzels.

"The hole in the wall was a rumor," says a uniformed Black man. He's tall, and he looks like he's in his twenties. "There's no evidence at all of any break in the perimeter. There is, of course, that slight weakness where Officer Belcher had his accident, but it was sufficiently patched up last month. Speaking of Belcher, we keep getting noise complaints. Can you tell him to turn down his music?"

"That's Agent Goodman," Elvis whispers in my ear. "He just got out of the academy, but my grandma thinks he'll run the FBAI one day."

"Roger that," Uncle Anish says.

"We did find something interesting in our last sweep of the west gate, though," Agent Goodman says.

"What is it?" Uncle Anish asks. He looks different here, more like he looked on that first day when I arrived. Stiff and official. Not like someone who would chat with a security guard about his niece's grades.

"Bubble Wrap. Lots of it. At least fifty feet. The good news is that whoever took the Zs was likely very careful. Made sure they wouldn't be punctured."

"Hmm," Uncle Anish says. "And still no ransom request, right?"

"Nope. That was my instinct too—that the kidnappers would make some sort of demand. But so far, nothing."

"Okay, please make sure we provide the Zs with extra patrols if they want them. I increased the security presence last week, but they might feel safer with more personal protection. We can't risk anyone else going missing. And bring that Bubble Wrap in. Let's check it for human DNA and prints and Break Through plasma."

"Already done. Brought it to the lab right away, and they found nothing."

"Seriously?" Uncle Anish asks. "Not even more Z pee?"

I almost start giggling, but I manage to keep it together.

"Nope. Are you thinking what I'm thinking?" Agent Goodman asks. I have no idea what either of them is thinking, but I sure hope it's not *I'm thirsty*.

My legs are starting to cramp behind this drinking fountain.

"Our suspect is likely someone trained in law enforcement. FBAI or maybe 51 police," Uncle Anish says.

"I need to call Washington, DC, stat," Uncle Anish says, and he doesn't look happy about it.

"*Stat* means 'immediately,'" Zane whispers to me. "My stepdad uses it all the time, like *Wash the dishes stat, Zane!*"

Uncle Anish pats his front pocket, as if to make sure that whatever he put there is safe and sound. When he moves his hand away, I see the blue top of my passport. Why does he still have it with him? What could he possibly need it for?

· · · THIRTY-ONE · · ·

A NOT-SO-GREAT HIDING SPOT

WE CRAWL OUT FROM BEHIND THE WATER FOUNTAIN A little dazed. I already knew that the Zdstrammars had likely been taken, but hearing that word, *kidnapped,* from my uncle himself makes me shiver. I think about that baby Z at the café. Is she in danger too? The thought freaks me out—I really liked those chatty Zdstrammars.

"We have evidence a Sanitizorian was at the west well recently," I say. "We should take a closer look at them."

"I don't see how they could capture the Zs," Elvis says. "And what would their motive even be?"

"They run all the golf cart washes in town. They are very good at their jobs," Zane says, apropos of nothing.

"You heard what my uncle said. Let's still keep them on our suspect list," I say.

"So what do we do next?" Elvis asks, looking from me to Zane. The hallway is empty, but we need to move quickly so we don't get caught. I shrug. I have no idea where we go from here. All I know is we need to find and rescue the Zs.

"I say we stick to our plan and sneak into the file room. See if we can dig up more information," Zane says. "Come on. It's this way."

We follow him, walking as fast as we can and sticking close to the walls. When we hear another agent round the corner, I grab my friends and pull them inside the nearest restroom to hide.

"Well, this is awkward," Zane whispers as we arrange ourselves around the gross toilet, trying desperately not to touch it.

"Sorry. I heard someone coming," I say.

Before I can start freaking out that I'm two feet away from where other people have recently dropped their feces, a siren starts blaring. This time it's *bingbingbing-bong, bingbingbing-bong.*

Red lights streak the room in a circle. It makes me dizzy.

"Oh no. We need to go now. We've been caught!" Elvis yells. I grab his hand, Zane grabs mine, and we burst out of the bathroom and sprint down the long hallway.

Feces is the scientific term for poop, dung, doodoo. In other words, what digested pizza eventually becomes.

"The cameras show three kids entering the building unauthorized. I think one of them is Agent Patel's niece." I can't see who is speaking—they are around a bend from our current hiding spot—but I don't recognize the voice. We're on the first floor, waiting for a chance to make a run for the door. The alarm is still blaring, and the place is swarming with agents. "When you find them, they need to be detained immediately. Do you understand?"

"Yes, sir," another agent says.

I've been holding out hope that the alarm has nothing to do with us—that maybe Elvis misunderstood the pattern, that there is some other emergency—but apparently no such luck. I really, really do not want to see what jail looks like in Area 51.

After the agents scatter, we stare wide-eyed at each other. The word *detained* sounds as scary as the word *kidnapped* did earlier.

"What are we going to do now?" Zane asks.

"I have a plan," Elvis says. "Do you trust me?"

Elvis

Also Elvis

THIRTY-TWO

LET ELVIS DRIVE THE BUS

I TRUST ELVIS, BUT HIS IDEA SEEMS TO BOTH DEFY THE LAWS of physics and require a whole lot of luck.

"I don't get it," Zane says.

"Most agents tend to see me as a large adult-sized male. If we can get the angles just right, I might be able to shield you with their perception of my bulk," Elvis says.

Elvis

Also Elvis

"Why do all the FBAI agents see you as a grown-up?" I ask.

"I don't know. Maybe something in their training? Maybe whatever instincts made them want to be an FBAI officer to begin with? Either way, it's never been a good thing, until now," Elvis says.

I remember how Officer Roidrage looked at Elvis when he caught us at the west gate, like Elvis was an enemy, not a kid. Like he was a real threat.

"So you want us to just stroll right on out of here?" I ask.

"Yup," Elvis says.

"And you think we can use your big body to shield us? But you're tiny!" Zane exclaims.

"Really? What do you see when you see me?" Elvis asks.

"You ever read those kids' books about the pigeon wanting to drive the bus? You look like that," Zane says.

"Are you saying you see me as a cartoon pigeon?" Elvis asks.

"I guess?" Elvis looks at Zane sideways.

"The pigeon is kind of cute," I say to lighten the blow. "And funny."

"The pigeon never gives up. Maybe that's why I see you that way. Because you always seem to be on some sort of mission. I think that's cool," Zane says, and it might be the first sort-of kind thing I've ever heard from Zane. I want to hug him because now Elvis is beaming.

"So you really think you can hide us?" I ask.

"I honestly don't know. But I think it's our only shot," Elvis says.

THIRTY-THREE

THE POWER OF OPTICAL ILLUSIONS

AND THAT'S HOW WE END UP STROLLING OUT OF FBAI headquarters. Elvis walks with the determination of the pigeon wanting to drive the bus, and based on the reaction of the guard working the exit, he must look like a big grown-up man to her. Not one of the three kids she's been told to look out for.

We stand to his right, hoping she can't see us. We make sure we all walk at exactly the same speed.

Amazingly, it works.

Elvis, again!

When we get outside, we can barely hear the alarms anymore. We run to the golf cart, not stopping once to catch our breath. When we climb in, we high-five and cheer, our faces aching from smiling so hard.

We did it!

A few seconds later, though, when the excitement of escaping starts to die down, we remember that we are still in deep, deep trouble.

"Okay, where to now?" Elvis asks, looking from Zane to me and back to Zane, but no one says a word.

"Maybe we should hide the cart behind some trees while we figure out a good plan?" I suggest a beat later. Zane and Elvis burst into nervous laughter. Right. Of course. We are in 51. Not a single tree for miles. "Or behind a building?"

"Didn't you say your grandma helped Sky? Should we go talk to her?" Zane asks.

"She'll call my uncle. We can't," I say.

"I'm pretty sure someone already notified your uncle. I mean, he is second-in-command of the whole FBAI. And he's going to become first-in-command at the medal ceremony in just a few days," Zane says, and my stomach drops. I'm in so much trouble. Back in California, I always followed the rules. I never once got a detention or had a teacher call my grand-mother or broke into a building or, you know, came anywhere close to going to jail.

What is it about this place that makes me take such big risks? I wonder if it has something to do with learning that the universe is so much bigger and fuller than I ever knew. Maybe knowing that has made me want my own life to be bigger and fuller?

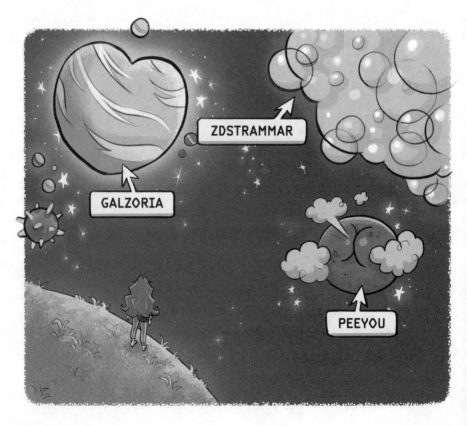

"I can't go home," I say.

"Agent Patel is on our side," Elvis says, pressing the button to start the ignition. "He can protect us."

"He'll shut us down. We need to find the Zdstrammars," Zane says.

"Zane's right. Either way, though, we need to get out of here right now," I say, because I hear the sirens starting up again in the distance and growing louder.

So. Many. Alarming. Alarms. In. Area. 51.

"Floor it," Zane says.

"What?" Elvis asks.

"Pedal to the metal," Zane says.

"Huh?" Elvis asks.

"Never mind," Zane says. "Just go FAST!" Elvis presses hard on the pedal and we go as fast as the cart can go. Which isn't all that fast. Still, it feels good to be moving forward, even if we have no idea where we should be going.

We head east, and the houses blur together in a pretty mess of pastels and fluorescents. Back in California, the houses were mostly white or beige or brown, as if everyone had a meeting and agreed to avoid the rest of the rainbow. For reasons I can't explain, this makes me sad. When we repainted Grandma's house to fix it up to sell, we never even considered a shade of pink.

While I'm on the subject of silly human rules, how come we never have cake for breakfast?

Elvis turns left down a narrow road, then right, and then left again. The sirens grow fainter with every maneuver. We drive into an area I haven't seen before—with a restaurant, a commissary/supermarket, and a hardware store—all still bright and cheery.

Finally, we can't hear the sirens.

"Wait!" Zane calls from the back. "Pull behind there."

Elvis expertly parks the golf cart behind a large trash bin, and a gross garbage smell wafts over us. This might be worse than the toilet at FBAI headquarters. Though it's still not nearly as bad as sitting next to a Peeyou.

"I keep thinking about the Bubble Wrap they found at the wall," Zane says.

"What about it?" I ask.

"Well, pretty much everything is rationed at 51, right? Like you can't just go buy new clothes, because we don't want deliveries coming in and out except on Drop Day. Families are supposed to take only what they can use, fix something when it breaks instead of replacing it, recycle when things can't be used in any other way. One of the basic tenets here is to minimize waste," Zane says. "Even that garbage bin has a solar panel."

"What does that have to do with the Bubble Wrap?" Elvis asks.

"Bubble Wrap is plastic, so it falls under 'severely restricted items.' The Zdstrammars get more of it for obvious safety reasons, but you can't just go to the store and buy a ton at a time, even if you are a Zdstrammar. They won't let you. So where did that extra supply come from?"

"Are you saying you think a Z did this because they had access to more Bubble Wrap?" Elvis asks.

"Uncle Anish said he thought that whoever did this was likely FBAI. Are any Zdstrammars FBAI?" I ask, piggybacking on Elvis's theory.

"I don't know. But even if they are, I don't think this means that it was a Zdstrammar. No single Z would be able to get enough Bubble Wrap," Zane says. The smell of rotting pizza moves through the cart, and my nostrils flare. I fight back a wave of nausea.

"What about Sanitizoria?" I ask.

"Nope. No one can. That's my point," Zane says.

"So the question is: How did whoever did this get the wrap?" Elvis asks.

"Exactly," Zane says.

"Never mind," I say. Of course no internet means no online shopping. Just thinking about it makes me itchy for my laptop. I miss being able to Google answers to any question. Like yesterday I was wondering about how light-years work, because Mrs. Moleratty keeps mentioning them at school, and I couldn't just look it up.

I'd ask Elvis, but my guess is he'll tell me to read the 51 handbook.

"Maybe they stole the wrap from the hardware store?" Zane asks, and points to the building in front of us.

"Couldn't hurt to go inside and ask, I guess," I say.

"Okay, but only two of us should go in. The other should stay and stand guard outside in case the FBAI come looking for us. This is the signal if we need to flee." Elvis pumps his arms in a circle, like he's cheering at a basketball game. "Who wants to go in?"

"Me! If I spend one more minute next to this garbage can, I'm going to hurl," Zane says.

"Me too," I say.

"Why?" Elvis asks.

"Because it stinks!" both Zane and I exclaim.

"Really? Galzoria don't have olfactory senses. Apparently the odor of sulfur is so strong on my planet, we've adapted to not smell anything," Elvis says. "To be honest, I don't even really understand what it means to smell. You feel a taste in your nose? How is that possible?"

"Let's just say right now you are very, very lucky," Zane says.

THIRTY-FOUR

LOOK HER IN THE EYE

I'M KIND OF EXCITED TO SEE A 51 STORE. FROM THE OUTSIDE, it looks like our local Costco, so I picture the inside like a giant warehouse. Wide aisles and little food sample stations. I could totally go for a mini–hot dog right now. Or ten.

Things I've learned today: running for my life makes me hungry.

For mini–hot dogs.

When we walk in, I'm immediately disappointed. There's only a counter staffed by one of the Picasso girls from my class. Not a free food sample in sight.

"Hey, Zane. Hey, Sky. Didn't realize you two were friends," she says. I stare at her chin, which is where her eyeball is, and then I notice she has another eyeball attached to her right hand. I keep forgetting to ask Elvis where is the politest place to look. Do aliens also have the custom of looking each other in the eye? Should I shift from chin to hand and back?

"Hey, Cubista," Zane says in a tone that's way friendlier than any he's ever used with me. I guess he's trying to butter her up.

Oooh, the word *butter* makes me think of cinnamon toast. Man, I'm hungry.

"The catalog is right over there," she says flatly, and points to a giant book that looks a lot like the 51 handbook.

"Anyone request Bubble Wrap recently?" I ask Cubista, trying to sound casual. Like asking about her previous customers is just chitchat.

"Don't think so. I don't pay much attention to what people buy, though. I type in the codes, and then you pick up your item from the door in the back. Why?" she asks.

"Just curious," I say at the same time Zane says "Sky needs some and thought she could do a trade."

Cubista narrows her eyes—both palm and chin—but doesn't say anything.

"Looks like you have pretty tight security here," Zane says, hands in his pockets, all *nothing to see here* stroll, and nods toward a security camera pointing right at our faces. I wonder how long we have before the we hear the sirens again. Does their security feed go straight to the 51 police department? I picture Uncle Anish zooming up in one of those super-speedy golf carts with Officer Roidrage alongside him.

I glance back at Elvis, who is outside the window. He flips me a peace sign. *All good.*

"Yeah," Cubista says, and she sounds bored. One of her eyes closes, so maybe she's not bored. Maybe she's tired.

The Picasso girls are hard to read.

"Heard you had a break-in a few weeks ago. Were you on duty?" Zane asks. He's surprisingly good at this. If he were this calm and friendly at school, I bet he'd have lots of people to sit with at lunch.

"That sounds scary," I say, playing along.

"Nah, where did you hear that? This place is a fortress. Harder to break in here than it is to break into 51, and you know how hard that is. You definitely heard wrong," Cubista says. "So what can I get you?"

"Um . . ." Zane flips through the book. "One R56JK98, please."

"Personal number?" Cubista asks, like she says this so often it repeats in her dreams. Wait, do Break Throughs dream?

"Resi 98302."

"Sorry. You've already used up your household plunger allotment. If you need yours fixed, you can head to the repair shop instead," she says, pointing to a sign on the counter that says *Let's Reduce, Reuse, Recycle 51 Times!*

"Oh right. Sorry. Thanks," Zane says, and we leave empty-handed.

No leads in the case and no mini–hot dogs, either.

Not even a nacho.

THIRTY-FIVE

WAFFLE FRIES ONLY

THERE IS ONLY ONE FAST-FOOD DRIVE-THROUGH IN ALL OF 51, and they only serve waffle fries. One day I will understand why this is—out of all the options, why this particular snack and only this particular snack— but today is not that day.

Area 51 raises so many more questions than it answers.

I wonder if Google even knows.

I doubt it.

Good thing I love waffle fries.

We pull up to the window in our golf cart, and Zane orders and pays with his personal number. We eat in a parking lot in the back. The cart is semi-shielded by the restaurant's sign, which has three words in all caps: WAFFLE FRIES ONLY.

"My parents' favorite thing to do is to come here and ask if they have curly fries. And when they say no, they ask all innocently, 'How about steak-cut?' And then they both crack up," Elvis says. "I don't really get it. The sign couldn't be clearer."

"Parents are weird," Zane says. "Though it's nice that yours laugh. I don't think my mom and stepdad like each other very much."

"I'm sorry," I say. I remember my passport sticking out of Uncle Anish's pocket and wonder what that means. When he finds us, which he *will* since he practically runs this place, will he put me on a plane and send me away? Where could I even go?

"It's okay. At least I have parents," Zane says, and then covers his mouth with his hands, looking ashamed. "Oh no, I'm so sorry. I didn't mean for it to come out like that. Sometimes I'm accidentally rude."

"It's fine. Really," I say. "I know you didn't mean anything by it."

"When I was little, I used to wish Blobby was my dad," Zane says.

"We're going to find him," Elvis says with a certainty I do not feel. I try to picture Blobby, but all I see is his backyard, the lonely Bubble Wrap flapping in the breeze.

"Wait a minute. Do all Zs wrap up their yards?" I ask.

"Yeah, most do. Why?" Elvis says.

"Well, maybe instead of stealing wrap from the store, our kidnapper stole directly from the Zs. Didn't Froth say something about not being a fan of the petty crime here? She could have been talking about Bubble Wrap!" I'm so excited by what feels like a breakthrough in the case (not a Break Through, as in an alien) that I fling a waffle fry right at Elvis's face. It bounces off his cheek.

"Ouch," he says, and throws one back at me. I'm not sure what comes over me—giddiness from being on the run from the law, maybe—but I take a handful and throw them at him. Soon we are in an all-out food fight.

We laugh so hard, tears streaming down our faces, that we somehow don't even hear the siren until right before Officer Roidrage pulls up right next to us.

THIRTY-SIX

SPIKE AND PICKLES, PICKLES AND SPIKE

I HAVE A WAFFLE FRY IN MY HAIR, OR POSSIBLY TWO, BUT I can't take them out because my hands are held together with handcuffs. Elvis is between me and Zane, also cuffed, and though he's frozen in exactly the same way he was last time we saw Officer Roidrage, he seems way calmer than Zane and I are. Like he hasn't yet imagined what will happen when we arrive wherever Officer Roidrage is taking us. I picture a dungeon, not unlike my uncle's hatch but without the awesome snacks and bathroom.

The three of us are stuffed into the two-person backseat of the police golf cart. Our elbows dig into each other's sides.

"My parents are going to murder me," Zane mutters over and over again.

"I've secured them, Agent Patel. I'll bring them in," Officer Roidrage announces into his walkie-talkie.

All police-ish. The way he sneers the *them* makes us sound like hardened criminals.

"Roger that," I hear my uncle respond. I try to read his tone, but I realize that I don't know my uncle all that well. I have no idea what he sounds like when he's angry. Or when he's happy, for that matter. I pretty much only know what he sounds like when he's stressed, which he's been since I arrived. I don't like that my coming here has caused so much trouble for him.

That's one of the strange things about being an orphan: You know that whoever ends up taking care of you didn't necessarily volunteer for the job. And that they might also change their mind at any time.

I assume kids with parents don't worry about being given away.

"If I go to jail, who will feed Spike?" I whisper to Elvis.

"First of all, relax. No one is going to jail. And don't worry, Pickles will take care of Spike. My mom told me they hang out when we're at school," Elvis says.

"Who are Spike and Pickles?" Zane asks, and it looks

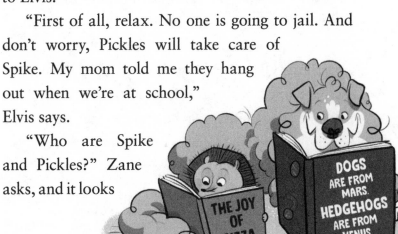

THE JOY OF PIZZA

DOGS ARE FROM MARS. HEDGEHOGS ARE FROM VENUS

like the deep breathing Elvis suggested is working. He seems way less shaky and pale. "They sound like a comic-book duo. Spike and Pickles to the rescue!"

"It sounds better the other way. Pickles and Spike save the day!" Elvis says.

"Spike is my hedgehog, Pickles is Elvis's dog," I say. "And whichever order you put them in, they have to be better crime fighters than we are." My nose itches, but when I try to scratch it, I end up slapping myself with the metal chain. "Ouch."

"Quiet back there," Officer Roidrage barks. Up close, his octopus tattoo looks even meaner than it did the first time I saw it. Like it could come alive and attack at any moment. What does it mean, and why would anyone would want to have ink injected into their neck, not to mention in the shape of a killer eight-legged mollusk?

Sometimes humans are way more confusing than aliens.

"Sorry," I squeak.

"I said QUIET!" he yells. This time we get the message and shut our mouths. For the rest of the ride, the only sound I can hear is my heart thumping hard in my chest. As alarming as an alarm.

THIRTY-SEVEN

AREA 51 PRISON?

OFFICER ROIDRAGE DOESN'T TAKE US TO FBAI HEADQUARTERS.
Instead, he takes us to the only building I've seen here that is not painted a happy color. It's a gray cement square, drab and cold-looking, despite the blaring desert sun. There don't even appear to be solar panels on its roof.

It looks exactly like what I assume it must be: a prison. Do they even have judges or juries here? Or do they just lock you up in jail and throw away the key?

"What is this place? I thought I knew every corner of 51," Zane whispers.

"No idea," Elvis says. "But I don't like it."

"It gives me the creeps," I say.

My uncle walks out the front door to get us. I can tell immediately that he's furious. He looks exactly like my grandmother used to when she was mad at me—shoulders back, spine stiffened. I used to joke that my making her angry was great for her posture.

"Get out, you three. Now!" he screams.

"They might make a run for it," Officer Roidrage says.

"Unlock them now!" Uncle Anish says through gritted teeth. My uncle is so mad he looks about seven feet tall. Officer Roidrage takes a key from his belt and unlocks me first. Zane next. Pauses for a minute at Elvis.

"Not all of them are kids," Officer Roidrage mutters, and I remember suddenly that he doesn't see Elvis the same way I do.

"Yes, all of them," my uncle says. "Give me that."

Officer Roidrage slowly walks over, gives Uncle Anish some sort of weird chest-thump bro hug, and hands him the key. My uncle steps out of his grasp, confused—I guess the bro-hug thing is new?—and rushes to unlock Elvis's cuffs. Then the three of us kids stand there, rubbing our sore wrists.

Of course Officer Roidrage made them super tight. They've left bright red circles on my skin.

"You know what, Officer? I can take it from here," Uncle Anish says, and tilts his head at Officer Roidrage's golf cart.

"I need to fill out an incident report back at the station anyway," Officer Roidrage says as he climbs behind the steering wheel, taking the hint.

Admittedly, it wasn't subtle. Even Zane would have gotten that message.

"There will be no incident report," my uncle says.

"What?" Officer Roidrage looks shocked.

"Just pretend this never happened or I'll report you for putting cuffs on three minors. Your job is to be a peacekeeper, not an aggressor. You know this is against guidelines," Uncle Anish says. I wonder if the guidelines are in the 51 handbook or if there is a whole other book for the police department.

Area 51 sure loves rules.

"I thought . . . ," Officer Roidrage says.

"You thought wrong. Now go." My uncle points to the dusty road, and Officer Roidrage zips away.

☢ ☢ ☢

We follow my uncle into the building, and I'm shocked when we go inside. It's not a jail after all, but a super-cool lab. Gloopy fluorescent liquids drip in gigantic floor-to-ceiling jars lined up along the walls. The counters are overflowing with beakers and microscopes and petri dishes and other science-y things.

"Is that . . . ?" Elvis asks.

"Yup. The very first alien aircraft to land here in 51 in 1947, and this is the very first building, where

this entire place started. There's been some debate about moving the saucer to the library, but the scientists who work here love it too much to part with it," Uncle Anish says. "Some even say it gives off positive energy, though that hasn't been proven."

"It's beautiful," Zane says reverently. He looks at the saucer the way I look at a bowl of ice cream and french fries.

"I've never seen anything like it. Where did it come from? Who came here first?" I ask, and Elvis and Zane both look at me as if I have two heads. Actually, that's not quite right. We've all seen aliens here with two heads and no one looks at them twice.

Man, I'd love to see a UFO landing in person.

"What?" I ask.

"I keep telling her to read the handbook," Elvis says to Uncle Anish.

"The Zdstrammars were the first alien life form to come to Earth," Uncle Anish says.

"Oh, right," I say.

"Everyone knows that," Zane says.

"Actually, 99.9 percent of the people who live on Earth do not know that," I say, and stick out my tongue. Uncle Anish rolls his eyes at us.

I'm still in very big trouble. This place might not be a jail, and he might have sent Agent Roidrage away, but that does not mean I am off the hook.

"I come here to think sometimes. Apparently I left headquarters about two minutes before your little stunt," Uncle Anish says.

"We didn't mean to trigger a manhunt," I say. "Or I guess a niece hunt."

"A Galzoria hunt!" Elvis says.

"I'm sorry," I say.

"Sit," Uncle Anish interrupts sternly, so we line up on lab stools, me between my two friends. I try to relax my face muscles to look extra innocent, but my forehead is too scrunched up. Like it's impossible to let go of the fear. "I don't want to hear another word. Elvis and Zane's parents will be here momentarily to pick them up and then you and I are going to have a little talk, Sky."

I look at my friends, and they look back at me, scared. My eyes fill with tears. I miss my grandma, who even at her tallest never felt this scary. For maybe the millionth time since I came to 51, I miss *home* and tacos and my life before it became so complicated. Before I understood that we shared our universe and our planet with other amazing life-forms, and that they are kind and bizarre and kind of bizarre and not so different from us.

Before I understood how fragile that secret was.

Before I understood what it means to have friends. How it is both a privilege and a responsibility.

Elvis takes my right hand under the table, and Zane takes my left, and they both squeeze a tiny pulse of encouragement. And just like that, I don't feel so homesick anymore.

· · · THIRTY-EIGHT · · ·

YOU HAVEN'T SEEN WHAT I'VE SEEN

"I GUESS YOU FOUND WFO," UNCLE ANISH SAYS AFTER ELVIS and Zane and their parents have left and it's just the two of us, sitting across from each other. The only other sound is an occasional gloppy boop from the jars.

"WFO?" I ask. I'm looking at my hands, because I'm too nervous to make eye contact.

"Waffle Fries Only," he says.

"Oh, right," I say, still confused. And then he reaches across and wrestles smooshed potato from one of my curls. "They were surprisingly good."

"Yeah. When your mom and I were kids, your grandmother used to take us to this diner near our house, and they had the best waffle fries," he says. "They had this flavor. I can't describe it."

"Seasoned salt," I say.

"What?"

"Seasoned salt. Grandma told me how she used to take you guys out for fries and she asked the owner what the secret spice was and he refused to tell her. She thought it might have been a racist thing. She figured it out a few years ago, though, when I accidentally bought seasoned salt instead of regular at the market. Now she puts it on everything. Seriously. Everything. Like even sneaks it into her chicken curry. She says it reminds her of the good old times, when you and Mom were little." I finally get the nerve to look up. Uncle Anish is staring at me with his mouth hanging open. "What?" I ask.

"I just . . . You look and sound so much like her," Uncle Anish says with tears in his eyes.

"Like who? Grandma?" I ask.

"No. Your mother. You look exactly like she did at your age," my uncle says, and his voice cracks. "She was my best friend. I miss her every day."

He takes a tissue out of his jumpsuit pocket and dabs at his eyes.

I don't say anything. I'm not sure I miss my mother, because I never got the chance to know her. But I miss the idea of her. I imagine that my entire body would feel different if I had a mom to tuck me into bed every night—fuller and warmer. Like wearing a winter coat inside my skin.

"Sky, all I want is to make sure you stay safe. I might have failed your mom, but I will not fail you," Uncle Anish says.

"But I am safe," I say.

"You could have been hurt today. This is serious. There's a kidnapper on the loose, who I'm pretty sure is out to get me, which means they could be out to get you, too. Look," he says, and points to his pocket. "I have your passport with me at all times now. Want to know why? It's because no one can take you without it. You need ID to leave 51, and even if they figured a way out of here, they couldn't cross any other borders with you." He hangs his head and rubs his bald scalp vigorously. I wonder if he thinks that will help grow back his hair.

"No one is going to take me, Uncle Anish," I say.

"You don't know that, Sky. You haven't seen what I've seen."

THIRTY-NINE

A VERY SMALL PRICE TO PAY

UNCLE ANISH ISN'T GREAT AT DISCIPLINE, BECAUSE INSTEAD of grounding me when we get home, he calls in a Code 61155, which is the same as a 61154 but with extra pepperoni. We sit out back under the night sky, the stars stretched above us like a painted ceiling. My uncle points out the constellations, and for a minute, I think about all the other alien civilizations, how on Galzoria, which is so far we can't see it from here, there are millions, if not hundreds of millions of Elvises. The thought makes me feel infinitesimal, like I'm just a tiny speck in the universe.

But it makes me feel less lonely, too.

I might be a speck, but I'm a speck woven into this spectacularly beautiful system's fabric.

"What's going to happen if we don't find Blobby and his friends?" I ask.

"You mean if *I* don't find Blobby and his friends. You are not finding anyone," Uncle Anish says.

"Right," I say, but keep my fingers crossed under the table. No way my friends and I are giving up now.

"I'll probably get fired. And then I don't know what will happen. I know too much to go back to the outside world. That's the deal you make when you come here," Uncle Anish says.

"How did you move here in the first place, Uncle Anish?" I ask.

"I moved here right after your parents died. I felt so sad and lost, and this place promised a bigger purpose. Saying goodbye to my old life, especially once your mom was gone, seemed like a very small price to pay to unlock the secrets of the cosmos."

He shrugs, takes another bite of pizza.

"Are we in danger?" I ask, and Uncle Anish starts coughing. I think his food went down the wrong pipe.

"Umm . . . I mean, I'm not sure what you mean by 'in danger,'" Uncle Anish says. "Or by 'we.'"

He doth protest too much, methinks.

"I mean are our lives at risk?" I ask.

"No, no, of course not. No. No. I, I, I don't think so," Uncle Anish says.

"Not going to lie. The number of noes you just used was not particularly comforting," I say.

"We're going to be fine, Sky. Promise."

"I'm sorry, sweetheart. I have to go," Uncle Anish says to me.

"Everything okay?" I ask. I don't hear any alarms. Despite the prickle of worry, I tell myself that no more Zdstrammars have been taken. We'd have to go in the hatch otherwise.

Uncle Anish pats his pocket to reassure himself my passport is still there, a gesture that is so automatic I'm not even sure he's aware he's doing it.

"Yup. Hunky-dory," he says, and flashes me a nervous smile before leaving.

FORTY

A GOOD TEAM

AFTER SCHOOL THE NEXT DAY, ZANE, ELVIS, AND I PICK UP Pickles and Spike on our way to the Zdstrammars' favorite café. I'm hoping this won't take too long, since I have Identifying Flying Objects and Understanding our Biosphere quizzes tomorrow that I have to study for. No offense to Yawn Middle, but my science teacher Mrs. Oodleboodlebaum knew absolutely nothing about astronomy.

She barely understood the basics of our little galaxy.

As Ms. Moleratty says, that's like if you were to study the human body and only focus on left pinky toenail cuticles.

"How did you end up with a hedgehog for a pet? It's a little weird," Zane says, and Spike goes full quill in response. Fortunately, he's riding on Pickles's back, so I don't get poked this time, but Pickles shimmies with pleasure.

"Don't worry, Spike. Weird isn't a bad thing," I say.

"Certainly not here in 51," Elvis says. Pickles barks in agreement and wags his fluffy tail. Today Elvis is a wearing a T-shirt with a picture of the three-taco special from my favorite Mexican place near the beach in California.

"My grandma used to work in a veterinarian's office, and someone found him abandoned on the side of the road. Brought him to the doctor in a shoe-box. He was only a tiny baby then, smaller than my palm. Anyhow, I took one look at him and I knew we were going to be best friends." Spike shakes his quills, which I think of as his preening dance. I reach out my finger and he rubs his tiny pink nose up against it.

"I want a pet, but my stepdad hates animals," Zane says.

"How can anyone hate animals?" I ask, and Zane shrugs.

"You'd be surprised. My stepdad hates a lot of things. Including me."

"I don't believe that," I say.

"Me neither," Elvis says.

"Why? *You* used to hate me," Zane says without anger. We're passing the library again, and I remember how I felt when I saw Zane's signature on the inside flap of that book. I was 100 percent sure he was our bad guy.

"*Hate* is a strong word," I say.

"And anyway, that was before we got to know you. I think you are super cool now," Elvis says.

"We make a good team," I say, and bump Zane's elbow. He bumps mine back, and Elvis throws an arm around the back of his neck. Zane's mouth curves into a smile.

"We do make a good team," Zane agrees. "Now let's go find Blobby."

♣ ♣ ♣

The Zdstrammars who gather here every afternoon look like they haven't moved since we last visited them. The mom and baby are still attached bubble to bubble. Froth floats separately from the pack. Their chatter is loud and piercing. I can hear them from a whole block away.

"You're back-back-back" Froth says flatly, and gives Spike the stink eye.

"Spike knows not to get too close. Don't worry. He wouldn't hurt a soul," I say. One of Froth's bubbles grows larger and smaller, and I take that as a nod.

"We're real sorry to bother you, ma'am," Zane says, both hands held aloft in peace signs, and I'm amazed how he's like Elvis in the way he's constantly morphing. With Zane, though, it's not his physical appearance that changes but his personality. This version of Zane is all charm. "We just want to ask a few quick questions."

"You're Blobby's friend-friend-friend," Froth says.

"Yes, I am. And I'm worried about him," Zane says. "Though I know he was with your wife, Pop, when he was taken, and I like to think they're looking out for each other."

"So you believe he was taken? Because your stepdad was here a few days ago asking all sorts of questions that made it sound like he thought they might have gone home-home-home," Froth says. "Which is simply nonsense. Not to mention impossible-ble-ble."

"I'm new here, so I'm sorry if this is a stupid question. But why is it impossible?" I ask.

"You humans have no understanding of how intergalactic travel works. Zdstrammaroos is hundreds of thousands of light-years away. It's not like hopping a plane to Paris-is-is," Froth says, and makes a sound that is identical to a snort, though I don't think she has an actual nose.

"I know they were taken. No way Blobby would leave without saying goodbye," Zane says.

"Who was the last person to see your friends before they went missing? Was it Officer Roidrage?" I ask.

"I suppose so. He checked them in for their shift-shift-shift," Froth says.

"And is there anything the three Zs who have gone missing have in common? Some reason why anyone would target them in particular?" Elvis asks.

"They were the ones who had gotten together to protest for more freedom," Froth says. "Whoever took them, I'm guessing, was not happy about those protests."

My stomach sinks. As far as I can tell, Uncle Anish is the only person who had reason to shut down the protests.

"We were curious . . . before the kidnapping, had anything been stolen from you? Did you have any other problems?" Zane asks.

"I did," the mom with the toddler bubble says. "We were given extra wrap when Snugglebug was born to baby-proof the yard. A few weeks ago, I came outside and it was gone. Poof. Just disappeared-d-d."

"Is that what you meant the other day when you mentioned recent petty crime?" I ask Froth.

"Yes. A bunch of our yards were stripped. Why anyone besides one of us would want Bubble Wrap is beyond me-me-me," Froth says. "What do humans need it for? You already have skin-skin-skin!"

"Any chance you have security cameras?" Elvis asks.

"Area 51 is literally the safest place on this entire planet. I've been here forty-seven Earth-years, and this is the first time we've ever had these sorts of issues," Froth says. "Until recently, I didn't even lock my front door-door-door."

"But don't forget about what happened to Blister," the mom reminds Froth. "He was popped-d-d."

"What happened to Blister?" I ask.

WHAT HAPPENED TO BLISTER:

BLISTER

"That was an accident. Most Zs are smart enough not to hang out with a knitter. Old humans can be quite dangerous with their fondness for those poky sticks-sticks-sticks," Froth says.

"Sharp things are not our friends," Snugglebug says, as if this is a mantra. Spike, who had already turned himself into a harmless ball, brings his quills in even tighter.

"You think there's a connection between the missing wrap and the kidnapping-ing-ing?" Froth asks.

"Yeah, we do," Zane says.

"I'll ask around again. See if anyone here saw anything-ing-ing," Froth says.

"Thanks," Zane says.

"Blobby always said you were a good kid. He'd be proud of you for looking for him-him-him," Froth says. Zane smiles and nods, his eyes just the tiniest bit teary.

FORTY-ONE

SOMETHING IS VERY WRONG

WHEN WE GET BACK TO OUR HOUSES, ELVIS'S PARENTS are waiting for us on the front lawn. Michael has his arm around Lauren's shoulder, and they both look like they have aged ten years since I saw them last. Lauren's hair, usually pulled back in a slick ponytail, is messy, and her face is streaked with black eye makeup. Michael's jumpsuit is unbuttoned and smeared at the shoulder with what looks like mucus.

Uncle Anish's front door is wide open, as if someone left in a hurry.

My chest feels tight.

Something is very wrong.

This feels even more alarming than the gazillion literal alarms that have gone off since I came here.

Even Pickles senses the shift in the air, and he lets out a sad howl. Spike climbs me until he's perched on my shoulder, and he nudges my cheek with his nose. A hedgehog kiss.

"What happened?" Elvis asks. He comes to stand behind me, which I appreciate, because I'm worried I might pass out.

"Sky, honey, we need to talk," Lauren chokes out, her voice shaky. "Let's go inside. I'll make you a cup of tea. Or maybe not tea. The caffeine will stunt your growth. How about milk and cookies?"

"Um," I say, looking back at my house.

"Where's my uncle?" I ask.

"That's what we need to talk to you about," Michael says. My eyes feel gritty and dry from the desert heat, and a ribbon of loneliness sneaks its way through my body like a chill.

I know without them having to say a word: my uncle is gone.

♣ ♣ ♣

We sit on Elvis's couch, and Pickles snuggles my feet, as if to warm them. Michael sets a tray on the coffee table, and Elvis grabs some cookies and stuffs them into his mouth. My stomach twists with nausea.

"Uncle Anish is dead, isn't he?" I ask. I can't wait another second. I need to know what's happening.

"No, honey! Of course not," Lauren says. "It's just that—"

"So he just left me. He left Area 51," I interrupt, eager to get this over with. To pull off the Band-Aid. I'm surprised to find I'm not crying. Instead, I feel like a computer that's been powered down. Empty, hollow, too slow to process anything.

"No. He'd never leave you. Not if he could help it. The thing is, he's been, um, well, he's been arrested," Lauren says. "He was taken into custody by the 51 police an hour ago and charged with the kidnapping of the Zdstrammars."

"What? But he didn't do it!" Elvis exclaims. Michael shrugs, like maybe he's suddenly not so sure, like it's totally possible that my uncle, who has been his neighbor for years, could be guilty of the crime.

"You'll be staying with us for the time being, while we figure this all out," Lauren says. "We've made up the extra bed in Elvis's room."

If circumstances were different, I'd normally be psyched for a sleepover with my best friend. At Yawn Middle, I was never invited to any slumber parties. But Elvis and I aren't going to pop popcorn and watch cheesy movies and practice TikTok dances.

I wonder if I should call Grandma—maybe she can help me out of this mess—but then remember there are no phones.

"Do you know why they arrested him? Do they have any evidence?" I ask. I am aware that I should thank them for taking me in, but I'm too numb. My voice sounds calm, almost normal. Like I'm talking about a television show and not my real life.

"They got a tip that your uncle had Pop's security badge. She was wearing it when she went missing," Michael says.

"Fartz!" I say, practically screaming, as all the pieces click into place. I feel like a real detective. "Fartz must have planted it at our house. That's why he came over. It's him. Zane's wrong—Fartz took the Zdstrammars!"

"Now, you can't go around pointing the finger just because you're worried about your uncle," Michael says. "That's not right."

"But . . . Fartz came to our house. It's him. I know it!" I yell.

"The thing is, sweetheart, the badge wasn't found in your house. It was found in your uncle's pocket," Lauren says.

"MY PARENTS THINK THESE ARE FUNNY," ELVIS SAYS, pointing to his sheets, which are decorated with aliens—or, at least, the cartoon Hollywood version. Little green men with antennae. "Every night, I sleep in a dad joke."

"Ha," I say, and close my eyes then open them again. For the first time, Elvis is wearing something other than a T-shirt. He has on matching long-sleeved pajamas decorated with pictures of his own face. I kinda want a pair. "Elvis?"

"Yeah, Sky?"

"What are we going to do?" I ask. I like Elvis's room. It's as homey as I would have imagined, with its night sky and fun sheets and the piles of books on the nightstand. But even its warmth can't seem to chase away the fear. "I'm scared."

"First thing tomorrow, we get Zane and the three of us will figure this out. I promise," Elvis says.

"You're not crossing any fingers or toes or anything, right?" I ask.

"Of course not. I don't even have fingers and toes," Elvis says.

"Okay," I say.

"We're going to figure out who did this and bring Agent Patel home, where he belongs," Elvis says. "I swear on my planet."

I look at his heart-shaped home, wondering if it's as hot there as it looks from here. I think about how far Elvis is from almost all the other Elvises in our universe.

I wonder whether that distance makes him lonely.

"Thank you," I say.

"That's what best friends are for. We have each other's backs, even if one of us doesn't literally have a back," he says.

"Can I ask you a question?" I ask.

"Always," Elvis says.

"What do you think about when you look up at the sky?"

"My parents. My biological ones, I mean. How they are gone but still here somehow," Elvis says. "And also how we are all, humans and Break Throughs, made of the same stardust."

"Yeah. Me too. Not the stardust thing, but the parents thing. Sometimes the sky makes me miss my parents more, and sometimes it makes me feel less alone," I say.

"Well, you, Sky, definitely make *me* feel less alone," he says.

"Good night, Elvis," I say as I hear his breathing relax into sleep.

Spikes curls up next to me on my pillow, and I spend the rest of the night that way: awake, staring at the ceiling and listening to the sounds of Pickles snoring.

FORTY-THREE

NEW PLAN

"NO WAY. I KNOW YOUR UNCLE DIDN'T DO IT," ZANE SAYS. "And I was the one who was convinced from the beginning that he was our guy."

"I know he didn't do it too," I say. "But we need to figure out who did."

We are in the cafeteria, because apparently in 51 you still need to go to school even when your uncle is arrested and thrown in jail.

YUM! Almost as good as pizza!

"How are you so sure it's not Agent Patel?" Elvis asks Zane once we're sitting at our table. "I one hundred percent agree, of course, but I'm curious about your deductive reasoning and certainty."

"Blobby used to say you can tell a lot about a person based on how they treat other people and Break Throughs," Zane says, like it's simple. "Even though he had a million reasons for being angry at us the other day, your uncle was still kind. Someone like that couldn't have taken Blobby."

"They're doing the medal ceremony tomorrow," Elvis says.

"The medal ceremony?" I ask. "Already?"

"Yup. To make Agent Belcher the head of the new FBAI. It was always planned for tomorrow, but it was supposed to be Agent Patel who was promoted. With your uncle in jail, though . . . ," Elvis says.

"Oh," I say.

"At least it's Agent Belcher, not Agent Fartz. No offense, Zane!" Elvis says. Zane shrugs, not offended, though in my experience the words *no offense* have always been followed by something extremely offensive.

"It's kind of a big deal around here. Whoever is appointed chooses the next head of the 51 police department, since they work so closely together. The current head is Officer Glamcop, and your uncle was likely going to reappoint her. They already get along so well. It's sort of like when a candidate for president picks her vice president," Zane says. "There's even a parade."

"Seriously?"

"Yup. It's kind of fun."

I give Zane a sharp look.

"I mean, obviously this one won't be," Zane adds.

"I need to go see my uncle. You think they'll let me talk to him?" I ask.

Elvis and Zane pick up their backpacks and drop their lunches in the trash, their movements perfectly coordinated, like they planned it.

"There's only one way to find out. Let's go," Zane says.

♧ ♧ ♧

It turns out I was wrong. You don't need to go to school when your uncle is unexpectedly arrested. Both Zane and Elvis are convinced that Ms. Moleratty is not going to punish us for skipping our afternoon classes given the circumstances. All I know is that at Yawn Middle we weren't allowed to skip for anything except dental appointments, and even then I needed to get a signed note from

Dr. Veneers. Elvis drives the golf cart south toward the prison, and we move through a neighborhood I haven't seen yet. This one is dingier than where Uncle Anish lives.

"What is this place?" I ask.

"This is where the Arthogus used to live. Before they went extinct," Zane says.

"They're not actually extinct," Elvis says. "They're just extinct on this planet."

"Right," Zane says. "You know what I meant."

"Sky, you still haven't read the handbook!" Elvis says, and grins at me in the rearview mirror.

"I've been a little busy," I say, and grin back. I feel a rush of gratitude that despite the fact that my life is falling apart, Elvis can still make me smile. "Please someone tell me without making me look it up: Who are the Arthogus?"

"They are the only alien life to come to 51 and attempt war. They wanted to colonize our planet. Obviously, they were unsuccessful," Zane says.

"It was messy here for a while," Elvis says. "You know Officer Roidrage's neck tattoo?"

"The scary octopus?" I ask, and both Zane and Elvis burst out laughing. "What?"

"That's not an octopus. That's an Arthogus!" Elvis says. "Officer

Roidrage led the charge against them. Most went back home willingly, but one got killed fighting back. Officer Roidrage claims he zapped him in self-defense. No one knows what really happened."

"And then he got a tattoo? That's so creepy!" I say.

"I know. My stepdad claims Roidrage saved one of the tentacles and had it taxidermied for his wall," Zane says.

"Ew," I say.

"He and Belcher are best friends, so I bet Roidrage'll be the new police chief. The Break Through community is really upset," Elvis says. "Which is another reason we need to get your uncle out of jail. If Officer Roidrage runs the police department, I don't know what's going to happen. He's one of those humans who came to 51 not because he's interested in other life-forms but because he screwed up his own life and needed to run away."

Who would've thought Belcher was best friends with Roidrage? I've seen the way Officer Roidrage looks at Elvis, and I felt how tight he clicked our cuffs the other day. If he becomes police chief, the Break Throughs are in trouble.

We pull up in front of the jail, which is fluorescent pink, like the school. It's a tiny building, though, not big enough to hold more than a few prisoners. This surprises me. Back in California, there was a correctional facility on the outskirts of town. It was larger than the community college.

We walk in the front door, and behind the security desk sits the old woman with the C-shaped back who hugged me at FBAI headquarters.

Oops. Really regretting forgetting to bring her those thank-you cookies right about now.

"Well, look who we have here," she says, and stares me down. She doesn't seem as warm and fuzzy today. She wears a name tag that says *Officer Betty White*.

"I'm so sorry about the other day, Officer White," I say. "We didn't mean to cause trouble. I'm hoping I can talk to my uncle?"

"See, that's how it's done. If you want access to someplace, you simply ask. You don't sneak your friends past," she says, and folds her arms across her chest.

"We really are sorry," Zane says, and steps out from behind me.

"Aww, you must be Zane, Agent Fartz's stepson! I've heard so much about you. So lovely to meet you!" She opens her arms for a hug, and Zane gets enveloped by her surprisingly long arms.

"Now, don't get any ideas," she says over Zane's

shoulders. "I have my eye on you three. I'll sign you in, Sky. I'm sure your uncle will be very happy to see you. You two will have to wait here, though. Follow me."

I follow Officer White down a short hallway, noticing that all the cells we pass are empty except the final one.

Officer White doesn't lock the door behind me.

It would be way too easy for me to break my uncle out of here.

· · · FORTY-FOUR · · ·
A NOT-SO-BAD PRISON

UNCLE ANISH SEEMS TO HAVE SHRUNK SINCE I LAST SAW HIM.
He stands, his bald head shiny with sweat. His cell
has a cot, a small table with books piled on it, and
a little bathroom attached. Not so bad, considering
it's a prison.

"Sky! I was so hoping you'd come," he says.

"Are you okay?" I ask. I don't know how to greet
him. Are we supposed to hug? We don't usually do
that. We are still so new to the roles of uncle and
niece.

"Fine. Totally fine. It's not too bad in here. When
Elvis's grandmother become head of the FBAI, she
remodeled the prison based on the Norwegian system. The idea is to treat everyone with respect, and
then criminals are less likely to commit more crimes.
Never thought I'd end up here myself, though."

"Yeah, visiting you in jail wasn't on my top ten

list of things to worry about when I first moved here," I joke, and he gives me a weak smile.

TOP TEN LIST OF THINGS TO WORRY ABOUT WHEN I MOVED TO AREA 51:

1. Aliens
2. Aliens
3. Aliens
4. Aliens
5. Aliens
6. Aliens
7. Aliens
8. Aliens
9. Aliens
10. Have I mentioned the aliens??

"I've been so worried about you," Uncle Anish says.

"You've been worried about *me*?" I ask, shocked, because surely Uncle Anish has bigger fish to fry right now. Like proving his innocence and getting the heck out of here.

"Of course! It's my job to worry about you."

And just like that, the tears that were nowhere to be found yesterday flood my eyes.

"I'm okay," I say, blinking too fast.

"Unfortunately we don't have much time. Here, take your passport. I think it's safer with you," he says, and gives me a meaningful stare. "Take care of it. Double-check that everything is there when you get home."

I didn't realize passports have parts that can fall out, but I nod and tuck it into my back pocket.

"Sure."

"You know I didn't do this, right? Tell me you know that," my uncle says.

"Of course I know that!" I exclaim.

"Phew. Go see Agent Goodman if you can. I'm pretty sure he's on my side. He'll help sort this out. And, Sky?"

"Yeah."

"I know I haven't been the greatest uncle so far, but I just wanted to make sure you understand that I love you very much. We'll get through this. I promise." I look at his fingers and his toes—he's still wearing his flip-flops—and sigh in relief when I see nothing is crossed.

He must really mean it.

FORTY-FIVE

A FEW THEORIES

WE SIT IN THE HATCH AT UNCLE ANISH'S HOUSE FOR MAXIMUM privacy. Elvis drags an old-fashioned blackboard downstairs, because all of history's greatest crime solvers scribble with chalk and then have great revelations. We don't get very far, though. After an hour, the only thing to show for our efforts is Elvis's pile of Snickers wrappers and random doodles.

"Okay, here's what we know. Someone stole Bubble Wrap from the Zs for the kidnapping, which they then timed perfectly with your arrival. Now the question is why," Zane says. He writes WHY on the board and underlines it three times. He then adds BUBBLE WRAP.

"They timed the kidnapping to frame Agent Patel," Elvis offers. "They knew Sky was coming and it would look suspicious."

Zane writes TIMING.

"But what's the motive? Why frame my uncle? Because they needed someone to blame?" I ask. "Or because they had their own reasons for shutting down the protests?"

Zane writes MOTIVE.

"I think whoever did it was jealous and angry about you coming here because they wanted to bring a relative over too and were denied," Elvis says. "So maybe it was an act of revenge."

Zane writes REVENGE.

"Guess that makes sense," I say, and shrug. It doesn't quite fit, because I can't see anyone hating my uncle enough to go to the trouble of framing him. But I guess it's the best explanation we have at the moment.

"What about the Sanitizoria gel? Could the Sanitizoria have something to do with this?" I ask. "Maybe they were at the west gate."

"Maybe," Zane says.

"Oh, I almost forgot! Uncle Anish told me to check my passport," I say, and take the little blue book from my back pocket.

"What does that mean?" Elvis asks. "Check your passport?"

"No idea," I say, but when I open my passport, a tiny yellow origami swan flutters out. I pick it up carefully and unfold it to find a note.

"Read it!" Elvis says.

Zane writes READ IT!

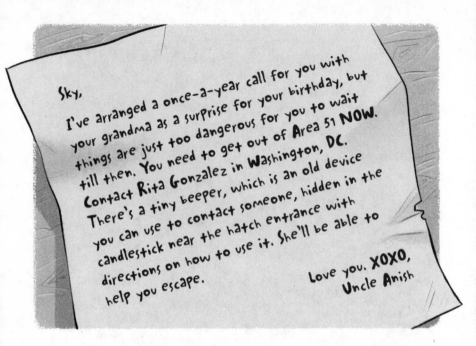

Sky,

I've arranged a once-a-year call for you with your grandma as a surprise for your birthday, but things are just too dangerous for you to wait till then. You need to get out of Area 51 NOW. Contact Rita Gonzalez in Washington, DC. There's a tiny beeper, which is an old device you can use to contact someone, hidden in the candlestick near the hatch entrance with directions on how to use it. She'll be able to help you escape.

Love you. XOXO,
Uncle Anish

"Rita Gonzalez is the secretary of defense," Zane says, and Elvis and I both look at him, shocked, since neither of us has ever heard of her. "What? The library gets a monthly news report and Blobby reads it to me."

I fold up the paper and tuck it back into my passport for safekeeping. I'm having too many feelings at once. I miss my grandma, but I'm not sure I want to run away. My friends need me. Uncle Anish needs me.

Elvis charges up the stairs.

"What are you doing?" I ask.

"Fartz! Remember, he was touching the candlestick. Maybe he took the beeper!" Elvis calls.

✿ ✿ ✿

Later, after we've done a celebratory dance, we get back down to business.

"I should contact Rita Gonzalez," I say. "And then I can ask my grandma what we should do."

"Do you want to leave 51?" Elvis asks.

"No, but this is an emergency!" I say. "We need her help!"

"How can she help all the way from California? We can do this together," Elvis says.

"We can," Zane says.

"Are you sure?" I ask.

"We're sure," Elvis and Zane say at the same time.

They're right. I don't need my grandmother's help. I don't need to leave.

We can do this. We can save Uncle Anish. We can save 51. Together.

And after all, my birthday is not so far away. I can be strong and brave until then.

"So I have a thought," I say, and Zane writes THOUGHT on the board.

"Zane, you don't have to write everything we say," Elvis says.

"Okay, so remember how your mom said that the evidence was found in my uncle's pocket? What if Roidrage dropped it in there outside the lab? Remember he gave Uncle Anish that super-weird bro hug? He could have snuck it in," I say.

"But they found it a whole day later. Agent Patel would have changed his jumpsuit since then," Elvis says.

"Maybe the badge fell between the pages of the passport and he switched it to his pocket without noticing. Like how I took the passport from the jail and put it in my pocket without seeing the note," I say.

Zane, of course, writes ORIGAMI/SECURITY BADGE.

"Interesting theory. That puts Roidrage at the top of our suspect list," Zane says.

"What about Fartz?" I ask.

"I told you he wouldn't do this," Zane says. "And anyhow, the badge wasn't found here. It was found on Agent Patel! My money is on Roidrage."

"He hates Break Throughs, he was the last person to see the missing Zs, *and* with your uncle out of the way, he's going to be the new head of the 51 police force," Elvis says. "That sounds like a motive to me."

"But Roidrage has a rock-solid alibi," I say.

"The 51 police station is right near the west gate. He could have checked the Zs in, followed them out, kidnapped them, and gone straight back to work," Zane says. "No one would have known he was gone."

"Let's go talk to Agent Goodman," I say.

FORTY-SIX

THAT DUDE IS THE WORST

WE FIND AGENT GOODMAN DOING AB CRUNCHES HANGING from a bar in the blazing sun in his full jumpsuit outside FBAI headquarters. Apparently there are no gyms in Area 51, because humans are the only life-forms that need exercise.

"This is how I get out my frustration," he explains, when he spots us waiting to talk to him. He hangs by one arm, using the other to flash his fingers in a peace sign. "You look just like your uncle, but with hair. Nice to finally meet you, Sky."

After my outburst about

We think it's Roidrage. Officer Roidrage kidnapped the Zs!

Officer Roidrage, Agent Goodman says, "You talk like your uncle, too. No sugarcoating. Straight to the point." He drops to the ground to face me and grins. "Now tell me your theory. Other than 'that dude is the worst,' because that's not new information."

We catch Agent Goodman up—how we are convinced that Roidrage dropped Pop's security badge in my uncle's pocket after arresting us—and surprisingly, Agent Goodman doesn't question our logic. Instead, he leads us to his golf cart—one of the special fast ones—and says, "Get in!"

And that's how we find ourselves peeking through the back windows of Officer Roidrage's house.

"He's on shift right now, so the place is empty," Agent Goodman whispers as we contort our bodies around the window so no one can see us. "Umm, you can get down now."

"Eww, more hand sanitizer?" I ask, seeing that I have more of that mucus-y gel on my sleeve.

"Don't worry about that," Agent Goodman says. "The Sanitizoria are responsible for cleaning all the windows in 51 and use their gel. It's biodegradable."

"Do they clean the walls, too?" I ask.

"Every day," Agent Goodman says. And just like that, my secret theory that maybe a Sanitizoria kidnapped the Zs goes up in smoke.

"So what's the plan? Break in?" Zane asks.

"Nope. I am a proud agent of the FBAI and would like to keep it that way. Here, take one of these," Agent Goodman says, and pulls a couple of devices from his backpack that look a lot like stethoscopes. "Our plan is to listen."

"Listen?" I ask.

"What's the defining characteristic of the Zdstrammars?" he asks, and if I didn't know any better, I'd think he was channeling Mrs. Oodleboodlebaum.

"They're bubbles and can be easily popped?" Elvis asks.

"Okay, their second defining characteristic," Agent Goodman says.

"They were the first species to come to 51," Zane says. "Nailed it."

Zane holds up his hand for a high five, but no one gives him one.

"Fine, their third defining characteristic," Agent Goodman says, a little annoyed.

"They are loud," I say. "When we went to the café I could hear them chattering a whole block away."

"*Ding-ding-ding,* we have a winner. If Roidrage kidnapped the Zs, he'd have to keep them somewhere private, right? Like his home? And if the Zs are here, we should be able to hear them chattering. Even if they are in the hatch. Even with a noise machine covering it up, we should still be able to hear something with these." We copy Agent Goodman and put the devices in our ears and hold the bases up to the windows. The only thing I hear is a television set, playing that same old newscast from 1951.

Hear anything?

No!

"They're not here," Agent Goodman says, and disappointment sits heavy on my shoulders.

I was hoping this would finally be easy.

We'd solve the case. Uncle Anish would be freed.

Tonight we could call in a Code 61155 and eat under the stars.

"What do you think you're doing?" a familiar voice shouts, and I go cold. There's Officer Roidrage, glaring at us with his hands on his hips, his tattoo flaring. Now that I know it's an Arthogus, I don't know how I ever thought it was an octopus. It's too angry-looking.

Did someone say Code 61155?

We instinctively line up behind Agent Goodman, though of course, Roidrage has already spotted us.

"Hey, Chuck," Agent Goodman says, all casual. Like it's not suspicious to find us holding stethoscope-like objects to Roidrage's house.

"I said, what do you think you're doing?" Officer Roidrage asks again. I didn't know his first name was Chuck. That sounds about right. He always looks like he wants to chuck something. Also, when I see him, I get the sudden urge to upchuck.

"Sorry, man. We'll leave. I put together a scavenger

hunt for the kids, to keep their minds off everything. Isn't it awful? Poor Sky over here. Orphaned, and now with her uncle in jail," Agent Goodman says.

"I wasn't born yesterday," Roidrage says. "You were spying. What were you hoping to find? The Zs?"

He barks a laugh so harsh and mean it's not a laugh at all. It's the opposite.

"Course not. Number six on the scavenger hunt list is barbells. Since they could tell you work out, the kids here thought they might be able to spy some through your window." Agent Goodman makes this sound so perfectly reasonable that I almost believe him. Even Roidrage smiles a little at the mention of his muscles, but then he catches himself.

"Get out of here. Now," Roidrage says. "And if I see any of you near my house again, there will be trouble."

He doesn't have to tell us twice. We scramble onto Agent Goodman's golf cart and speed away.

· · · FORTY-SEVEN · · ·
A CELEBRATION

ZANE WASN'T JOKING ABOUT THE PARADE FOR THE MEDAL ceremony. The square in front of FBAI headquarters is decked out with flags matching the mural on its wall: an image of an alien reaching an antenna into a human's palm. A marching band on a stage plays "Yankee Doodle Dandy." All of 51 is here—alien and human alike. I smell popcorn and cotton candy, and rumor has it fireworks are planned for later.

This is a huge deal.

Even Officer White is here, dancing with a man who looks as bent and old as she is but who is also as surprisingly spry. Elvis's grandmother takes the stage, and she seems commanding in her FBAI jumpsuit and a blue baseball cap. A fearless leader. The kind of woman I'd want to be in charge of everything except baking.

I can't bring myself to clap. This shouldn't be happening. We shouldn't be celebrating a new FBAI head unless it's my uncle.

I think about him all alone in his cell.

"Sky! Sky-Sky-Sky!" someone whisper-yells, and I turn to see Froth in what looks like a Bubble Wrap coat covering her circles.

"Large group gatherings are dangerous for us-us-us," she says, explaining her strange getup. "But I wanted to show you this-this-this."

She thrusts a little square screen into my hands, and at first I have no idea what I'm looking at.

"What's this?" I ask.

"You remember Snugglebug? The little Z you met at the café? Her mom uses an old recycled security camera as a baby monitor when she naps in the yard. Turns out it records the footage. She caught the Bubble Wrap burglary on tape-tape-tape!" I squint at the small screen. I see the back of a head, a glimpse of a neck, lots of shadows. "That's him. That must be who took Pop."

Elvis and Zane move closer and take a look too.

"Oh my snoogles!" Elvis says.

· · · FORTY-EIGHT · · ·

AN INCRIMINATING NECK

"BUT THE Zs WEREN'T AT HIS HOUSE. WE CHECKED!" I SAY,
squinting again. Still, there's no doubt about it. The
neck shows the tip of a tentacle: Roidrage's Arthogus
tattoo.

"So Roidrage's keeping them somewhere else,"
Zane says.

"It is my duty today to introduce to you the next
head of the FBAI," Elvis's grandma announces from
the stage, and though I detect a note of sarcasm, the
crowd doesn't seem to. They erupt in cheers all over
again. At least, some of the humans do. The aliens
look less enthusiastic. I can't blame them.

"Wait a minute," Elvis says, and grabs my hand,
his eyes growing large. "The noise complaints!"

"What are you talking about?" Zane asks.

"Remember, Sky? When we found Fartz at your
house and my grandmother told him to tell Belcher

to keep his music down. And Agent Goodman mentioned it too, I think. Belcher must have them! He's keeping the Zs!" Elvis says.

"Agent Belcher? The dude who looks like a Troll?" I ask.

"We were wrong about their motive!" I exclaim, and point to the stage, where Elvis's grandmother is making a big production of taking a giant gold pin from a box to put on Belcher's jumpsuit. "This is why they wanted to frame my uncle. So they could run 51! Come on! We have to stop them!"

I bound up to the side of the stage, and for a moment I feel cold move through my body. But it's not fear; it's just Chill getting in my way.

"Watch it!" he calls.

"Sorry!" I say over my shoulder as I take the steps to the stage two at a time. Elvis and Zane are right next to me, keeping pace. I see Elvis's grandma pick up the pin, about to place it on Belcher's chest.

STOP!!!

A hush falls over the crowd.

All eyes turn to me, and with this group, which has quite a few Retinayas, there must be at least a million. Literally. The crowd is even bigger than I would have guessed—an amazing collection of all shapes and sizes. Like seeing the posters on the wall of Uncle Anish's hatch come to life. I'm so stunned by the view I pause for a second.

"Can I help you, dear?" Elvis grandma says to me with a twinkle in her eye. She does not seem bothered in the least that we have crashed this ceremony.

"It's him! Belcher! He's working with Roidrage," I say, grabbing the microphone so everyone can hear me. "They took the Zdstrammars!"

I hold my hand up in a peace sign, and slowly I see the audience mirror it right back. They quiet down and wait to hear what I have to say.

"Come on. These kids just want a little attention. Get off the stage," Belcher says, attempting to grab the pin from Elvis's grandmother's hands. She holds on to it firmly.

"Tell us more, Sky," she says, and gives Officer White and her dance partner a discreet hand signal. From the corner of my eye, I see them unclip handcuffs from their belts.

"Here! Look! This is a baby monitor from a Zdstrammar yard, and you can see it's Roidrage stealing the Bubble Wrap. And didn't you say the

other day that Belcher's neighbors have been complaining about loud music? He's playing it so they don't hear the chattering of the Zs. I bet if we go to his hatch right now, we'll find them," I say.

"This is ridiculous," Belcher says. "I'm now head of the FBAI and I appoint Officer Roidrage as 51 police chief, and I hereby order you to stand down unless you want to join your uncle in jail."

"You will do nothing of the sort," Elvis's grandma says. "Betty, help me out here."

Officer White glides over.

"I say, before I pin you and make this official, we do a little recon mission first. You live only a block from here, right? Well, something smells a little sour about all this, Belcher," Elvis's grandma says, barely containing her laughter at her joke. "Come on, everyone. Let's take a trip to Belcher's house." To Officer White, she quietly adds, "Restrain Belcher and Roidrage, please. If we're wrong, we'll release them ASAP."

"But we're not," Elvis says, and his grandma winks at him.

We walk as a group to Belcher's house, a quiet procession of hundreds of humans and aliens on a shared

mission. I feel nervous, not nearly as certain as Elvis that we will find the Zs.

Maybe Belcher moved them somewhere else.

Maybe we have it all wrong. It definitely wouldn't be the first time.

Maybe someone else in 51 also has an Arthogus neck tattoo.

"Look who came to see this," Elvis says, and I hear a bark. Pickles's tail is wagging, and Spike sits on his back at full, happy quill. As we get closer to the house, you can't miss the music. The *Hamilton* soundtrack is playing at top volume. At least he has good taste in musicals.

Elvis's grandma takes the lead and uses a key from her belt to open the front door.

"She has a master key to all the houses," Elvis says, and shrugs. We follow her inside, and soon the house is crammed with 51 residents. I see an old-fashioned music player—I think it's called a CD player?—and I hit the stop button. The music cuts out, and then we hear them.

Chatter, chatter, chatter.

Froth bursts into noisy tears.

"They're here-here-here!" she screeches. Someone has already turned over the television, and someone else enters the code to the hatch, and the door is opened.

"Everyone get back," Elvis's grandma says. "Let's make room."

The crowd parts and Froth floats to the front. Three Zdstrammars, of varying numbers and sizes of bubbles, make their way up the stairs. One zooms into Froth, and they stick together, fused completely at their sides. That must be Pop.

Blobby zooms over to Zane. Zane lifts a finger and Blobby gently pushes his bubble against it. I guess this is how Zs hug non-Zs. Agent Fartz, who I didn't even realize was here, rushes to Zane and throws his arms around his stepson.

"You okay, buddy? You kids solved this all on your own? I'm so proud of you, Zane!" Agent Fartz says, and looks so genuinely happy to be hugging his son that I make a secret vow to myself: I'll stop with the fart jokes for a few toots.

No, for reals, I'm done.

You won't get wind of any more fart jokes from me.

They are all *behind* me now.

About an hour later, my uncle, newly freed from Area 51 prison, is onstage getting his pin. The crowd, still thrilled from earlier, cheers so loudly that even the Zs' chatter is drowned out.

"Meet your new FBAI chief, Agent Anish Patel," Elvis's grandma announces, grinning so widely I can see her cavity fillings.

Oh no. That means there must be dentists in Area 51. I hoped I'd get out of my yearly cleaning.

"And I'm pleased to announce the reinstated head of the Area 51 police force, Officer Glamcop," Uncle Anish says, and Officer Glamcop comes running up onstage. But before she can make it to the mic, she is tackled to the ground by the still-handcuffed Officer Roidrage, who somehow breaks free from Officer White.

"That's *my* job!" he screams. "You know how hard it was to get that Bubble Wrap?"

"Yeah, and you think kidnapping Zdstrammars was so easy? They pee everywhere! My jumpsuit is all stained. And they don't shut up!" Agent Belcher screams as he follows Roidrage onto the stage. He looks so different now, angry and out of control. Like a rabid dog. "Give me that pin! I earned it!"

Officer Glamcop jumps up and easily restrains Officer Roidrage in a headlock.

"No luck, Chuck. Do not pass go. Do not collect two hundred dollars. Go straight to jail!" she says in the mic. "Sorry, got an old Monopoly game at the last Drop Day! Been waiting for a chance to say that for a whole year!"

Uncle Anish has somehow managed to get Agent Belcher pinned on the ground, though his hair is still sticking so high up it reaches my uncle's knees.

"Please escort them both to jail, Officer White,"

Uncle Anish says, so calmly you'd think he was asking her to change the channel on the television.

Officer White and her husband grab Belcher and Roidrage and march them away.

"Hello, 51!" Uncle Anish says turning to the crowd, and they cheer. My uncle looks like a rock star onstage. Completely unrattled by the Roidrage-and-Belcher kerfuffle. "We have all our friends and neighbors here safe and sound. Now let's celebrate!"

And though this moment is too classified to find its way into the history books, something unexpected and amazing happens: I find myself in the center of the most epic human and alien dance party to ever occur on planet Earth.

· · · FORTY-NINe · · ·
THE SECRET BUTTON

THE NEXT MORNING, MY UNCLE DECIDES TO DRIVE ELVIS AND
me to school. Apparently, solving the biggest crime in
Area 51 history doesn't mean you get to play hooky.

"Buckle up," my uncle says, and then pushes a
button I've never noticed before under the steering
wheel of his golf cart. An engine revs and the cart
rushes forward, going at least sixty miles an hour.

"No way," I say.

"Are you kidding me? There's a secret button?"
Elvis says, thrilled.

"And if I ever catch either of you pressing it, you
are in serious trouble. I just thought you deserved a
little treat after saving my derriere," my uncle says.

"It wasn't Fartz!" Elvis says, smiling. "No more
butt jokes."

"But Belcher was full of hot air," I say, laughing.

"Let's not talk about him. He makes me want to

throw up in my mouth a little," Uncle Anish says, and we all crack up.

"Excuse me," Elvis says, mimicking the sound of a human burp.

We whoosh through the streets of 51, Uncle Anish dressed in his finest uniform, the same one he was wearing the first time we met. His shiny new FBAI pin is proudly displayed on his chest. Seeing it and knowing that Elvis and I had something to do with getting it for him fills me with pride.

We pull up to school, and as Elvis and I step out of the golf cart, I hear a strange sucking sound. I look up, and what looks like a tornado—or at least what a tornado looks like in comic books—hovers over our heads. The sky hollows, as if being vacuumed open.

"Oh my snoogles," Elvis says.

"Holy cannoli," I say. "What is that?"

My uncle licks his finger and holds it up to the air.

"I'd say we have some new visitors," he says.

"Really?" I ask. According to Elvis, you never forget the first time you see a UFO landing. I've been dying to see one.

"This is a rare one. Based on the wind pattern and the shape, I'm pretty sure they're from Galzoria," Uncle Anish says, grinning. I look at Elvis, who is wearing a T-shirt with a picture of himself, Zane, and me. He's smiling so big I wonder if his face could split in half.

I bend my head back so I can take it all in: the great big universe, this tiny glimpse into just one of its many beautiful secrets. Some new arrivals that change everything.

Suddenly, I understand my name in a way I never have before. Because looking up at the sky right now, I've never felt less alone.

THE AREA 51 FILES
SERIES CONTINUES WITH . . .

THE BIG FLUSH

Don't miss Sky's next
out-of-this-world adventure,
coming summer 2023!

ACKNOWLEDGMENTS

Thank you so much to Hannah Hill and the rest of the amazing Delacorte Press/Random House Children's Books team, and to my agent extraordinaire, Jennifer Joel. Forever thank you to Elaine Koster and Susan Kamil.

Thank you so much to Lavanya Naidu for bringing this book to life with your amazing illustrations!

This book was written during the pandemic, and I am so grateful for my writer crews for helping me get through. Special thanks to Charlotte Huang, Kayla Kagan, and Amy Spalding, who are always down for finding the perfect joke. Huge shout-out to Rose Brock, Max Brallier, Stuart Gibbs, Gordon Korman, Sarah Mlynowski, James Ponti, Melissa Posten, and Christina Soontornvat for showing me that the mg world is where the cool kids are. And thank you to my oldest and closest friends and family for always being there for me. You know who you are.

Thank you to Ayla and Emiana Slocum for your wild imaginations and alien suggestions. Thank you to Indy Flore, who I still not only love but like even though we've spent the last year locked in a house together. Extra special thank-yous and love to Luca, who gave me the idea for this book, and to Elili, who made this book better. ILYTTMABABABAI.

© INDY FLORE

UFO:
Unidentified
Food Object

JULIE BUXBAUM is the *New York Times* bestselling author of the young adult novels *Tell Me Three Things, What to Say Next, Hope and Other Punch Lines, Admission,* and *Year on Fire.* She also wrote the critically acclaimed *The Opposite of Love* and *After You.* She lives in Los Angeles with her husband and two children.

JULIEBUXBAUM.COM

satyam agarwala

LAVANYA NAIDU is a children's book illustrator and animator, born and raised in Kolkata, India. Over the last decade she has illustrated numerous children's books while also working on multiple animation productions for television and film. She served as head of design and episode director on the animated kids' series *The Strange Chores* (season 2) at 12field Animation. In her spare time, Lavanya enjoys collecting dinosaur models and befriending dogs!

@Lavanyanaidu